She had said that she would marry him...now, she was beset with any number of doubts.

"Thank you for dinner and for bringing me back," Alethea said politely, and then felt foolish at his reply.

"I hardly think that you need to thank me, my dear. Such small services will be my privilege in the future."

"Oh, yes, of course." She smiled a little shyly at him, and then in a burst of confidence added, "You know, when I got up this morning I'd made up my mind to say no."

"And what made you change your mind?" he asked quietly.

"I haven't the faintest idea." She smiled a little. "But I won't change it again."

He took her hand, bent his head and kissed her—a quick, light kiss, which, although it had meant nothing at all, stayed in her mind long after she had wished him good-night and had gone to bed.

Romance readers around the world were sad to note the passing of **Betty Neels** in June 2001. Her career spanned thirty years, and she continued to write into her ninetieth year. To her millions of fans, Betty epitomized the romance writer, and yet she began writing almost by accident. She had retired from nursing, but her inquiring mind still sought stimulation. Her new career was born when she heard a lady in her local library bemoaning the lack of good romance novels. Betty's first book, *Sister Peters in Amsterdam,* was published in 1969, and she eventually completed 134 books. Her novels offer a reassuring warmth that was very much a part of her own personality. She was a wonderful writer, and she will be greatly missed. Her spirit and genuine talent will live on in all her stories.

THE BEST *of*

BETTY NEELS

SUN AND CANDLELIGHT

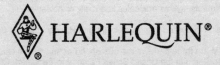

HARLEQUIN®

TORONTO • NEW YORK • LONDON
AMSTERDAM • PARIS • SYDNEY • HAMBURG
STOCKHOLM • ATHENS • TOKYO • MILAN • MADRID
PRAGUE • WARSAW • BUDAPEST • AUCKLAND

ISBN-13: 978-0-373-19883-2
ISBN-10:   0-373-19883-3

SUN AND CANDLELIGHT

This edition published by arrangement with Harlequin Books S.A.

® and TM are trademarks of the publisher. Trademarks indicated with ® are registered in the United States Patent and Trademark Office, the Canadian Trade Marks Office and in other countries.

www.eHarlequin.com

Printed in U.S.A.

The man opposite her glanced at her angrily and then looked away. 'You're such a fool, Alethea—everyone goes away for weekends these days, why not you? Think yourself too good?' His voice held a sneer, his good looks marred by a frown. 'You couldn't have imagined that I was going to ask you to marry me? Lord, it'll be years before I get a consultant's post—I can't afford a wife, certainly not one without any money.' He smiled suddenly and added coaxingly: 'Come on, be a sport.'

The waiter served them and retreated again. 'I must be the most unsporting girl for miles around,' observed Alethea calmly, and then somehow stayed calm as he suddenly got to his feet and without another word, walked away, hurrying between the tables so that people paused in their talk to stare at him. He went out of the restaurant without a backward glance and after a moment Alethea took up her spoon with a hand which shook slightly and started on her sorbet. She would have liked to have got up and left too, but the awful re-alisation that she had no more than a handful of small change in her purse prevented her. Presently the bill would be handed to her and she wouldn't be able to pay it, and it hardly seemed likely that Nick would come back. She spooned some more sorbet and swallowed it with difficulty; she mustn't cry, which was what she wanted to do very badly, and she mustn't look around her too much—and above all she mustn't appear anxious. She ate slowly, putting off the moment when the bill would arrive; she could spend at least fifteen minutes over her coffee, too; perhaps by then Nick would come back, although she was almost certain that he wasn't going to.

She had agreed to dine with him with such high hopes too. They had been going out together for some months now; the whole hospital expected them to get engaged, although she had never even hinted at it and she was sure now that Nick hadn't either. She had even bought a new dress for the occasion; a fine black voile patterned with a multitude of flowers, its low neckline edged with a narrow frill and its high waist tied by long velvet ribbons. It had cost her more than she could afford, but she had wanted to look rather special for what she had expected to be a special occasion. After all, Nick had told her that he had something important to ask her and she, fool that she was, she thought bitterly now, had expected him to propose. And all he had wanted was a weekend at Brighton.

She put down her spoon; she had spun out the sorbet just as long as she could… She made the coffee last too, aware that those sitting at nearby tables were glancing at her with some curiosity and presently the waiter presented himself discreetly. 'The gentleman is not returning? Madam will wish to pay the bill?' He laid the plate with the folded bill on it beside her and withdrew again, and after a minute Alethea plucked up the courage to peep at it. The total shocked her, and how was she going to pay it? Even if they allowed her to go to the hospital by taxi and fetch the money, where was she going to get it from? It was almost the end of the month, neither she nor any of her friends had more than a pound or two between them, and the banks, naturally enough, were closed. She stared stonily ahead of her, picturing the scene which was going to take place within the next few minutes. She would die of shame and she would never, never forgive Nick.

She had been attracted to him on the very first occasion of their meeting several months ago now; he had come to Theobald's as Orthopaedic Registrar and they had seen a good deal of each other, for she was Sister in charge of the Orthopaedic Unit. She had admired his dark good looks and his obvious intention to make his way in his profession and she had been flattered when he had singled her out for his special attention. Until she had met him she had never wanted to marry any of the men who had taken her out. She had had no very clear idea of what the man she would marry would be like; he was a dim, scarcely thought-of image in the back of her mind and she had known, even when she found herself attracted to Nick, that he bore no resemblance to that image, but that hadn't mattered; he had been attentive and flatteringly anxious to see as much of her as possible, but it was horribly apparent now that she had been mistaken about him. She shuddered strongly and felt sick and ashamed that despite the way he was treating her she still wished with all her heart that he would come in through the restaurant door at that very moment. And she would be fool enough to forgive him.

She closed her eyes for a moment and then opened them because she could feel that someone was looking at her. It only took her a second or two to see who it was; she hadn't looked around her until then; she had

been happily engrossed in Nick's company and hadn't
noticed anyone or anything else, otherwise, she had to
admit, she couldn't have failed to see the man staring
at her now. He was sitting to one side of her, sharing a
table with a pleasant-looking couple and facing her. He
was massively built with dark hair already greying at
the temples and a strong good-looking face. She
couldn't see what colour his eyes were in the one swift
glance she gave him before turning her head away with
what she hoped was cool dignity. It was a pity that this
move meant that she looked straight at the waiter, who
started towards her, obviously under the impression
that she was about to pay the bill. She sat up a little
straighter; in seconds he would be beside her, and what
on earth was she going to say or do?

The man who had been staring must have moved
very fast; he was there, standing in front of her, completely at ease, as the waiter came to a halt.

'Well, well,' he boomed in a genial voice, 'how delightful to see you again—I was coming over sooner,
but I quite thought that you were dining with
someone…' He looked and sounded so genuinely
puzzled that she almost believed him.

His gaze swept the table. 'You've had coffee? What
a pity, I intended asking you to join us. You're waiting
for your companion, perhaps?'

Alethea felt her jaw dropping and stopped it just in
time. 'Yes—at least, I think he may not be coming
back—I'm not sure… I…' Her eyes beseeched him to
understand; he looked kind and he gave every appearance of being a safe port in a storm. Normally she

wouldn't have allowed him to pick her up, for this was what he seemed to be doing, but every minute's delay helped; Nick might come back...

He had picked up the bill and put his hand into his pocket. 'In that case, shall I settle this for you? He can owe it to me until we meet next time.' He put some notes on to the plate and gave the waiter a cool look and then smiled at her. 'I'll see you home,' he said easily. 'My friends are leaving anyway,' he added quite loudly, 'it is so long since we last saw each other we should find plenty to talk about.'

Alethea managed a feeble yes and wondered why he had raised his voice and then saw that the people at the tables on either side were listening, so she smiled and said: 'Oh, yes,' and then heaved a sigh of relief. Once outside she could explain to him and thank him for helping her out of a nasty situation; he must have seen Nick getting angry with her and then leaving; it was a miracle that no one else had. The waiter smiled and bowed as she got up and went to the door, her lovely head high, very conscious of the man towering over her. He waited in the small lobby while she got her coat and then accompanied her outside into the April evening. They had walked a few paces along the pavement before she stopped and looked up at him.

'That was most kind of you,' she said in a voice made wooden by embarrassment. 'If you would let me know your name and address I'll send you a cheque first thing in the morning.' And when he didn't answer her she went on a little desperately: 'He—he said he had to leave suddenly—so unfortunate. He's a surgeon—he quite forgot about the bill…' Her voice tailed off into an unbelieving silence, and suddenly, staring up into the calm face lighted by the street lamp, she couldn't contain herself any longer. Rage and humiliation and fright boiled up together and combined into a sob. Worse, her eyes filled with tears and she, who almost never cried, was unable to stop them rolling down her cheeks. She wiped them away with an impatient hand and said in a voice made high by her feelings and the hock she had drunk with her dinner: 'That's not true— he left because I wouldn't spend the weekend with him at Brighton.' She hiccoughed. 'I thought he was going to ask me to marry him.' Her voice rose even higher. 'I bought a new dress!' she wailed.

Her companion didn't smile, he looked at her gravely and spoke just as gravely. 'It is a very pretty dress.' The way he said it made it sound like a delightful compliment. 'I'm going to call a taxi and take you back to wherever you want to go. A hospital? You mentioned that your—er—companion was a surgeon.'

Alethea gave a great sniff. 'Yes—Theobald's, but there's no need for you to come with me, I'm quite all right now, and thank you very much…'

'Nevertheless if you can bear with my company, I shall accompany you, Miss…er…?'

'Thomas. Alethea Thomas.' She took the handkerchief he was holding out and dabbed at her face. 'But what about your friends?'

'They were about to leave anyway, we were saying our goodbyes…' He lifted an arm and a taxi slid in to the kerb. 'I think a cup of coffee on the way might be a good idea.' He gave some directions to the driver as she got in and then got in beside her. 'I asked him to pull up at the next coffee stall we pass.'

They sat in silence until the taxi stopped and the driver enquired if that particular stall would do.

'Very well, and pray join us.' So that Alethea had a double escort across the pavement, the two men chatting easily about the latest boxing match. Really, she thought, she might just as well not have been there, only to find herself mistaken; she was seated carefully on a stool and the taxi driver mounted guard over her while her rescuer fetched three thick mugs of rich coffee and then engaged her in undemanding conversation in which the taxi driver joined, carefully not looking at her puffy face and both of them standing so that no one else there could get a good look at her. Not all men were beastly, she reflected.

Neither man seemed to be in a hurry, and it was a good twenty minutes later when they climbed back into the taxi, and by then Alethea's face was almost normal and although she still felt dreadful she was hiding it successfully enough behind a calm which matched her companion's. They were almost at the hospital when she said: 'I don't know your name.'

'Van Diederijk—Sarre van Diederijk.'

'Oh, Dutch. Your English is perfect...'

'Thank you.' The taxi had stopped and he got out, spoke to the driver and started to walk with her to the side entrance across the forecourt. She stopped then to protest. 'I go in at that door, thank you. I can walk through the hospital to the Nurses' Home.' She put out a hand, but he didn't shake it as he was meant to, but held it firmly and began to walk on again. 'I'll see you to the Home,' he observed, and took no notice of her murmur.

It was late, but not as late as all that; the night staff were still settling patients for the night; Alethea recognised the familiar sounds as they crossed the hall and started down a long corridor running towards the rear of the hospital; the soft hurried tread of the nurses, the squeak of trolley wheels, the telephone, the vague subdued murmur of a great many people as ward doors opened and closed. She turned a corner, Mr van Diederijk hard on her heels, and felt his hand close on her arm at the same moment as she saw Nick coming along the corridor towards them. He was still in his dinner jacket, strolling along, a cigarette in his mouth. He looked as though he hadn't a care in the world until he caught sight of them. He paused then and for one moment Alethea thought that he was going to turn round and go back the way he had come. But he thought better of it, hurrying past them as though he had something urgent to do, glancing angrily at her as he went.

'Your companion of this evening?' asked Mr van Diederijk mildly.

Alethea said yes in a miserable little voice. For a split second she had hoped that Nick would stop; she conceded that to apologise before a complete stranger would be a great test of his feelings for her, but it seemed that she wasn't worth it. Her companion's voice was very comforting. 'In that case how fortunate that I happened to be with you.'

She saw at once what he meant. If Nick had seen her creeping back on her own her mortification would have been complete, as it was he had been left to wonder just how she had replaced him so quickly...

At the narrow door set in the wall at the end of the corridor she put out a hand. 'You've been very kind, I can't thank you enough. And please give me your address so that I can send you a cheque in the morning.'

He went on holding her hand in an absentminded fashion. 'Ah, yes—I'll leave it at the porter's lodge as I go, shall I?' His smile was very kind. 'I'm glad that I could be of service—such a small thing, really, you know. And don't worry; these little differences are bound to crop up; they seem terrible at the time, but probably by the morning he'll be on his knees to you.'

She gave him an earnest look. 'Oh, do you really think so? But he did say...'

'People say the strangest things at times,' he pointed out in his placid way so that she felt instantly lulled into a more cheerful state of mind. He opened the door then and held it while she went through. Alethea bade him a final, rather shy goodnight and went down the badly lighted covered passage to the Nurses' Home door, not looking back.

She hadn't expected to sleep, but she did, although she shed a few tears first, but Mr van Diederijk's certainty that Nick would come to his senses in the morning had taken a firm hold on her unhappy mind. When Nick had apologised and everything was as it had been, she would tell him about it, and she must write a little note with the cheque, too, because Mr van

Diederijk deserved all the thanks he would get. If she saw Nick first, he might want to add a letter of his own as well as his cheque. She nodded her head into the pillow and closed her eyes; everything was going to be fine in the morning.

It was nothing of the sort. She overslept for a start and flew down to her breakfast, neat as a pin in her uniform and little white cap but with no make-up on at all and her hair caught up in a bun from which curly ends were already popping out. But in a way it was a good thing because there was no time for any of her friends to ask questions about her evening out. She gulped down her tea, bit into as much toast as she could manage, and went on duty.

The Orthopaedic wing was on the top floor at the back of the hospital, its windows overlooked a network of dull streets lined with brick villas long since divided into flats or let out as bedsitters. Alethea often wished that the unit could have been at the front of the hospital which overlooked a busy city street beyond its narrow forecourt, for at least the buses gave a spot of vivid colour to the view. She walked briskly into her office, consoling herself with the thought that if she hung out of its window she could just see Big Ben.

The night staff nurse was waiting for her, as was her day staff nurse and such of the nurses who could be spared to listen to the report—rather a lengthy one as it happened, for there had been admissions during the night; two young boys who had collided with each other, the one in a souped-up sports car, the other on a motorbike. Both were badly injured, one already back from theatre and the second due to go for surgery in the next ten minutes or so.

Alethea received this news with her usual serenity, together with the information that old Mr Briggs had taken a turn for the worse, Mr Cord's left leg, encased in plaster, presented all the signs of restriction to its circulation and would need to be dealt with pretty smartly, and last but not least, the part-time staff nurse who should have been coming on duty that morning had telephoned to say that her small boy had the measles.

'Things could have been worse,' remarked Alethea philosophically to Sue Phipps, her staff nurse, and ten minutes later wished the remark unsaid when the telephone rang to say that there was a compound fracture of tib and fib coming up and that the Orthopaedic Registrar would see it right away. Alethea, giving competent instructions as to the patient's reception, found time to wonder what Nick would say when he saw her. Would he ignore her, treat her as though they hadn't quarrelled or behave like a man wishing to apologise? She hoped it would be the latter and while she superintended the conveyance of the new boy to theatre, a small part of her mind was deploring the fact that she had had no time to do anything at all to her face. There was no time now, of course; no sooner had he been borne away than the latest patient was wheeled in. He had already been dealt with in the Accident Department, but only his leather jacket and jeans had been removed, together with his boots. Alethea, helped by the most junior of her nurses, was prising off the rest of his garments when Nick arrived. He didn't wish her good morning, only demanded her services in a curt voice and then wanted to know in an angry way why the patient wasn't already undressed.

'Because he's just this minute arrived,' Alethea pointed out sensibly, 'and he's not in a condition to have his clothes whipped off. His BP's down and his pulse is rapid—a hundred and twenty. His left pupil isn't reacting to light.' She spoke in her usual quiet voice and pleasant manner while her heart raced and thumped and her knees shook; Nick might have treated her abominably, but she was still in love with him. It remained to be seen if he felt the same about her; at the moment it was impossible to tell, he was being terse, almost rude, but perhaps he was worried about his patient.

The examination took a long time and in the end Sir Walter Tring, the orthopaedic consultant, joined them as he was on his way to theatre. The leg, he observed brusquely, was a mess, it would need pinning and plating, provided they could find all the fragments of bone. 'Wiring, too,' he went on thoughtfully. 'We'd better have him up after the lad who's in theatre now.' He looked across at Alethea. 'Keep you busy, don't we, Sister?'

She said 'Yes, sir,' cheerfully, and asked at what time the patient was to go for operation. The boy was unconscious still and there was a drip already up and as far as she could see, most of the cleaning up would have to be done in theatre. 'Put him on quarter hour observations, Sister,' Sir Walter ordered. 'I should think in about an hour's time, but I'll be down again.' He glanced at Nick. 'Penrose, check on that first boy we saw to earlier on, will you, and let me know his condition. I shall want you back here in about half an hour.'

He wandered off, not looking at all hurried—indeed, thought Alethea, watching him trundle through the ward doors, he looked like some nice easy-going elderly gentleman on his way to the lending library or a quiet game of bowls. Very deceptive; he could rage like a lion when peeved and wield the tools of his profession with an expertise which could shame a man half his age. He terrified her nurses too, but she herself was made of sterner stuff; she took no notice at all when he bit her head off for something or other which nearly always had nothing to do with her, and accepted his apology afterwards in the spirit in which it was given. They were great friends; completely impersonal, very professional towards each other while sharing a mutual regard.

Nick Penrose was writing up the boy's notes, not looking at her at all; she might not have been there. A little spark of temper flared in her, refusing to be doused by her love; he was behaving as though she had been at fault, not he. She felt a little sick, knowing that if he were to ask her to marry him she would say yes, despite the fact that tucked away right at the back of her mind there was the certainty that she would never forgive herself if she did.

He went presently, without saying a word and she set about the business of preparing the patient for theatre with the help of a student nurse and then made a hasty round of the ward. There was the boy in theatre, and the boy who had been admitted with him was as well as could be expected, but old Mr Briggs was another cup of tea. She pulled the screens round his bed and sat down, just as though she had all the time in the world, and talked to him; his wife would have to be telephoned straight away because he wasn't going to last the day. She left him presently, sent one of the nurses to make him comfortable and keep an eye on him, and telephoned Mrs Briggs before going to look at Mr Cord's leg. And that plaster would have to come off, she decided silently, looking at the purple foot beneath it. She went away to telephone the houseman, told Staff to get the cutters and shears ready and everything needed to replaster the limb, and glanced at the clock. The half an hour was up, had been ten minutes ago; she hurried down the ward once more, still contriving to look unhurried, and cast an eye over the boy. There was no change in his condition, so she sent the nurse to get her coffee so that she would be able to take him to theatre, and checked his pulse. She was charting it when Nick returned, took the chart from her without speaking and bent over the boy. He straightened almost at once.

'Who was that lazy-looking type you were with last night?' he wanted to know.

She hadn't expected him to ask, not now when they were so busy. She said shortly: 'Someone who very kindly saw me back—you owe him for the bill—he paid it.'

He stared at her with angry eyes. 'If you imagine I'm going to pay for your dinner, you're mistaken—and you found someone easily enough to pick you up, didn't you?'

'Hardly that,' said Mr van Diederijk. He had come quietly through the curtains and was standing just behind them both. 'I don't make a habit of picking up young women, nor, for that matter, do I leave them to pay for their own dinner.' His voice was quiet, but— there was a sharp edge to it so that Alethea judged it prudent not to say anything at all and Nick, trying to bluster his way out of an awkward situation, said too quickly: 'This is hardly the time or the place…'

'Too true, I'm glad you realise that,' agreed Mr van Diederijk equably.

'Who are you?' began Nick, and stopped as Sir Walter slid his bulk round the curtains in his turn.

'My dear chap,' he boomed cheerfully, 'nice of you to come along. This leg—if you can call it that at the moment—it seems to me that you're just the man to consult. A classic example of the kind of thing you excel in, I believe—wiring, I should imagine, and then intensive osteopathy to the femur to prevent muscle contraction—am I right?'

The question was rhetorical; Sir Walter was very well aware that he was right. Alethea said nothing, Nick muttered some answer or other and Mr van Diederijk agreed placidly.

'Yes, well, in that case, since we are agreed and you happen to be here I'd be delighted to have the benefit of your skill. A pity that you and that brother of yours don't have a clinic over here, but I daresay you get all the work you can cope with.'

'Indeed, we do. I shall be delighted to give any assistance I can.'

'Good, good. Sister, we'll have him in theatre in half an hour, please. Have you written him up, Penrose?

Yes? Very well, check on that boy I've just done in theatre, will you—and I shall want you for this case. Sister, is there anything worrying you or can you cope?'

'Mr Cord's plaster has had to come off—it's being re-plastered now—I got Mr Timms to see to it. Mr Briggs is… I've sent for his wife. The boy you operated upon during the night is satisfactory—there's nothing else, sir.'

'Good girl. Lean heavily on Timms if you need help and if that's not enough, give the theatre a ring.'

'Yes, sir. Would you like coffee?'

'Yes. Mr van Diederijk will too, won't you, Sarre?'

The big man inclined his head gravely. 'We are not delaying Sister?'

'Me?' she smiled at him, forgetting her rather pale unmade-up face and screwed-up hair. 'No, not at all. Mary, our ward maid, will have the tray ready, she's marvellous.'

She led the way down the ward and into her office, saw the two gentlemen served and then excused herself. The boy had to be got ready for theatre and over and above that, the routine work of the ward mustn't be halted.

When she went back to her office presently for an identity bracelet the two men had gone and presently the porters came and Alethea, sending her most senior student nurse with him, despatched the patient to theatre, before turning her attention to the work waiting for her. She had the time now to wonder at the sudden and unexpected appearance of Doctor van Diederijk; had he taken up an appointment at Theobald's? She frowned and shook her head as she adjusted the weights on Tommy Lister's pinned and plated leg, suspended from its Balkan Beam. No; she would certainly have heard about that, and yet he knew Sir Walter. Staying with him, perhaps? Over in England for some seminar or other? Now she considered the matter, he looked well-established, as it were, self-assured in a quiet way, and wearing the beautifully tailored garments which proclaimed taste and money, however discreetly. Perhaps he was someone important in his own country—and hadn't Sir Walter said something about a clinic and a brother? She let out a great sigh of frustrated curiosity and Tommy, who had been watching her face, asked: "Ere, Sister, wot's got inter yer? Yer look real narked.'

'Me? Go on with you, Tommy. Who's coming to see you this afternoon?'

'Me mum. When am I goin' 'ome, then, Sister?'

'Not just yet—I can't bear to part with you.' She laughed at him then, patted his thin shoulder, told him to be a good boy, and went on her way. He shouldn't have been in the ward at all, but Children's was full, as usual, and there was no point in trying to move him there even if there was a bed free, the business of moving him and his paraphernalia would have been just too much. Besides, the men liked him, he had a sharp cockney wit and he was always cheerful.

The day wore on. The boys who had been admitted during the night were picking up slowly; the patient of that morning had come back from ITU only half an hour since, still poorly, and his mother, fortified with cups of tea in Alethea's office, had been able to sit with

him for a few minutes. The boy had made a brave show
for that short time before, his anxious parent gone,
Alethea gave him an injection to send him back into the
sleep he needed so badly.

The ward was settling down into its early evening
routine and she was due off duty when Nick came
again. He had been down already to check Sir Walter's
patients, but beyond giving him any information he had
asked for, they had nothing to say to each other, but this
time, after a quick look at his charges, he didn't leave
the ward but followed her into the office where she was
writing the bare bones of the report, so that Sue, due
on in ten minutes or so, would have a little more time
to get finished before the night staff appeared. She sat
down at her desk and picked up her pen and gave him
an enquiring look.

He hadn't bothered to shut the door and he was in a
bad temper. 'Look here,' he began, 'I still want to know
how you came to pick up that fellow.'

She eyed him calmly although her heart was
thumping enough to choke her, and despised herself for
longing for him to smile just once and say that everything was all right again, that he hadn't meant a word
he had said…

'I didn't. He saw you leave and I suppose he guessed
that I might not have had enough to pay the bill—and
I hadn't—you might have thought of that. I don't know
what I should have done if he hadn't helped me.' She
paused. 'Nick—do we have to quarrel…' She hadn't
meant her voice to sound so anxious; she caught at the
tatters of her pride and was glad of it when he snapped:

'Quarrel? I'm not quarrelling, I've other things to do than waste time on a prissy girl like you…'

'I cannot agree wholly with you,' remarked Mr van Diederijk from the open door. 'Indeed, if there were the time, I would suggest most strongly that you should eat your words, but it is true that you are wasting your time, Mr—er—Penrose; they are looking for you in the Accident Room, I believe.' He glanced at Nick's bleep which he had switched off and now switched on again with a muttered grumble, not looking at anyone. And when he turned to go out of the door, Mr van Diederijk made no effort to move. 'A quick apology to Sister?' he suggested with a smile which Alethea, watching fascinated, could only describe as sunny, and Nick, furious, turned again and mumbled something at her before brushing past the other man. When he had gone there was silence for a few moments; Alethea was fighting to regain her calm and her companion seemed happy enough just to stand there, looking at the various notices pinned on the walls.

Presently Mr van Diederijk asked gently: 'Off duty, Sister?'

She wanted to pick up her pen, but her hand was shaking. All the same she achieved a very creditable: 'In about ten minutes or so, sir.'

'Then may I beg you to take pity on me and come out to dinner?' He sighed loudly. 'London can be a lonely place for a foreigner.'

She was in no state to care what she did or where she went; she supposed that she might just as well go out with him as spend the evening in her room, which was what she had intended to do. All the same, she was too nice a girl to make use of him. 'You might enjoy yourself better on your own, I'm not very good company,' she pointed out.

He shrugged huge shoulders. 'We don't need to talk unless we want to.' He smiled suddenly. 'Anyway, it might be better than spending an evening in your room, without your supper.'

Her fine eyes flew to his face. 'How did you know…?' and when she saw that he wasn't going to answer her question: 'Well, thank you, yes, I'd like to come.'

'Good. Half past seven at the entrance, then?' He turned as Sue came in, wished her good evening, passed the remark that he mustn't interfere with the giving of the report, asked if he might take a quick look at the boy who had been operated upon that morning, and went quietly away.

'He's nice,' breathed Sue. 'I could go for him in a big way. He'll be married, of course, the nice ones always are.'

'I don't know,' said Alethea, not particularly caring. 'Everything's fairly quiet; you'll need to keep an eye on that boy and the two who came in last night, I gave them some dope at five o'clock, but they'll need another lot to settle them. They're written up PRN and Mr Timms will be down before eight o'clock, so let him know if you're not happy. As for the rest…'

She plunged into a quick account of what had happened since Sue had gone off duty at dinner time, put her desk tidy and stood up to go off duty herself. It had been a horrid day, thank heaven it was over. Not quite over, though; she still had the evening to get through, but perhaps in Mr van Diederijk's restful company it would go swiftly. She sighed as she made her way through the hospital; she was sure that he was a very nice man, but he wasn't Nick. Nick—whom she ought to hate and despise instead of loving.

beautifully tailored, and his shoes were the sort that one didn't notice, but when one did, one could see that they were wildly expensive, too. He turned as she reached him and she realised that he had seen her reflected in the glass of the doors. His greeting was pleasantly matter-of-fact and his glance friendly but quite impersonal. 'Delightfully punctual,' he murmured, and opened the door for her to go through.

There was a car parked close by, a Jaguar XJ-S, gun-metal grey and upholstered in a pearl grey leather. He ushered her into it, got in beside her and drove out of the hospital forecourt. 'Do you know Le Français?' he asked as he turned the car's elegant nose into the evening traffic. 'I had wondered if we might go out of town, but you look tired—it's been rather a day, hasn't it? Perhaps another time—You like French cooking?'

He rambled on in his quiet deep voice so that all she had to do was murmur from time to time. Alethea felt herself relaxing; she had been right, he was a delightful, undemanding companion. She found herself wondering if she was dressed to suit the occasion; she hadn't taken very great pains and he had said that she looked tired, which meant, in all probability, that she looked plain. He cleared up the little problem for her by observing: 'You look very nice, but then of course you are a beautiful girl, even when you're tired.'

He spoke in such a matter-of-fact way that she wasn't sure if it was a compliment or a statement of fact. She said 'Thank you,' and then: 'It has been a busy day.'

They discussed it easily and at some length without being too serious about it until he parked and walked her across the pavement into the restaurant. It seemed that he was known there; they were greeted with a warm civility and when she had left her coat and taken a dissatisfied look at herself in the cloakroom, she found him waiting for her in the tiny foyer, talking with a man who she guessed might be the proprietor.

The bar was small but cosy and she was given time to choose her drink; she had become so accustomed to Nick ordering a dry sherry that for a moment she had to think. 'I don't really care for dry sherry,' she told her companion. 'What else is there?'

'Dubonnet?' he enquired placidly, 'or how about a Madeira?'

She chose the latter and when the barman had served Mr van Diederijk with a gin and tonic, she took a sip of her own drink. It was nice, and even nicer because she had been asked what she would like and not just had a glass handed to her. They sat side by side, talking about nothing much and deciding what they should eat; soup with garlic, Barquettes Girondines for Alethea and Entrecote Bordelais for her companion. She sat back feeling more peaceful than she had done since the previous evening, while he chose the wines.

Getting ready for bed, much later, she found herself unable to remember just what they had talked about; they hadn't hurried over their meal, and she paused in her hairbrushing to drool a little over the memory of the zabaglione and then worried because the memory of its deliciousness was so much sharper than their conversation. It was just as she was on the edge of sleep that she realised that she hadn't thought about Nick at all, not once they had started their meal. Simultaneously she remembered that Mr van Diederijk had suggested that they might go to a theatre one evening. She had accepted, too, with the sudden thought that perhaps if Nick heard about it, he might feel jealous enough to discover that he was in love with her after all. She woke in the night with the clear recollection of the under-standing in Mr van Diederijk's face when she had accepted his invitation.

Alethea was half way through her breakfast the next morning when she paused, a fork half way to her mouth. How could she possibly have forgotten to pay Mr van Diederijk the money she, or rather, Nick, owed him?

Her friends stared at her. 'Alethea, what's up? You look as though you've remembered something simply frightful,' and someone said cheerfully: 'She's left the weights off someone's Balkan Beam…'

There was a little ripple of laughter and Alethea laughed with them. 'Much worse!' but she didn't say more, and they, who had guessed that something had happened between her and Nick, carefully didn't ask what it was.

She would be bound to see him within the next day or so, perhaps even this very day, Alethea decided as she set about the business of allocating the day's work, but she didn't. There was no sign of him. Sir Walter came surrounded by his posse of assistants, talking to Nick, discussing his cases, but of Mr van Diederijk there was no sign. Alethea, with a half day she didn't want, took herself off duty and spent it washing her hair, writing letters and going for a brisk walk through the rather dingy streets around the hospital. She might just as well have taken a bus and gone up to Oxford Street and at least gone out to tea, but she had no heart for doing anything. Nick hadn't bothered to look at her during the round, and it dawned on her painfully that he really had finished with her, that he had meant it when he had declared that he wasn't going to waste time on her. He had called her prissy too. The thought roused her to anger, so that she glared at a perfectly blameless house-wife, loaded with shopping, coming towards her on the pavement.

She walked herself tired and returned in time for supper at the hospital, and her friends, seeing her bleak face, talked about everything under the sun excepting herself.

'That charmer's gone,' observed Philly Chambers, a small dark girl who was junior sister in the orthopaedic theatre. 'Much in demand he was too, and I'm not sur-prised—he should have been a film star.'

'You mean that giant who was wandering round with Sir Walter?' asked Patty Cox, senior sister on Women's Surgical. 'Very self-effacing despite his size, never used two words when one would do. I hear he's in charge of some new hospital in Holland where they combine or-thopaedics with osteopathy; surgeons and osteopaths work hand in glove, as it were. Sir Walter's interested, that's why he's been over here. He's coming back...'

'You know an awful lot about him,' commented Philly, and looked across at Alethea. 'You're the one who ought to know all the gen, Alethea,' she cried, and went on unthinkingly: 'Nick must know all about him…' She stopped, muttered: 'Oh, lord, I'm sorry,' and then: 'I'll fetch the pudding, shall I?'

Alethea had gone rather pale, so that her already pale face looked quite pinched. She said in an expressionless voice: 'I don't know anything about him,' and realised that she only spoke the truth; he had told her nothing of himself, indeed, she could remember nothing of their conversations, perhaps she hadn't been listening… She added: 'He seemed very nice, though.'

There was a little burst of talk with everyone doing their best to change the conversation. There had been a good deal of gossip about Alethea and Nick Penrose. No one had actually found out exactly what had happened, but the hospital grapevine was loaded with rumours. That they had quarrelled was a certainty and it looked as though their romance was at an end, judging from Alethea's face and unhappy air. Besides, Sue had told the staff nurse on Women's Surgical, who had told Patty in her turn, that Nick Penrose was ignoring Alethea when he came on the ward; he had always had coffee with her after his round in the mornings, and they had smiled a good deal at each other and although their conversations had been brief anyone could have seen that they were wrapped up in each other—but not any more. Besides, Patty had seen with her own eyes Nick strolling down the theatre corridor with the theatre staff nurse, a pretty girl who made no secret of the fact that she was out to get a member of the medical profession as a husband. He had looked remarkably carefree and pleased with himself too.

She finished her pudding, saw that Alethea had merely spread hers round her plate, and suggested that it might be worth going to the rather dreary little cinema a stone's throw from the hospital. 'There's that film on that I've been longing to see,' she declared, 'but I won't go alone—Alethea, keep me company, there's a dear, and what about you, Philly?'

She gathered a handful of friends round her and by sheer weight of numbers persuaded Alethea to accompany them. It was unfortunate that on their way out they should meet Nick Penrose, arm in arm with the theatre staff nurse.

Alethea went home for her days off at the end of the week, travelling down to the little village near Dunmow in her rather battered Fiat 500 on Friday evening, happy to shake off the hospital and its unhappy memories for a time at least. Once clear of London and its suburbs, the newly green and peaceful Essex countryside soothed her feelings. She had purposely left the main road at the earliest moment and had kept to the narrow lanes. It took a good deal longer, but the evening was a pleasant one and although she had told her grandmother that she was coming she had mentioned no special time. She reached Great Dunmow about seven o'clock and took the country road which would lead her eventually to Little Braugh, resolutely thinking about anything and everything except Nick. She had been a fool, she reflected, quite unable to keep to her resolution; Nick was an ambitious man and she had nothing to offer him but a pretty face and the qualities of a first-class nurse—he would want money too, for without that he would take twice as long to reach the top of his profession, and, whispered a small voice at the back of her head, Theatre Staff Nurse Petts was the only daughter of a rich grocer. She shook her head free of its worrying and concentrated on the road. But Nick's image remained clear behind her eyelids and no amount of telling herself that she was well rid of someone who had had no real regard for her could dispel it.

But there was no sign of her worrying when she drew up outside a small cottage on the edge of the scattering of houses which was Little Braugh. It was a pretty little place with a hedged garden and a brick path to its solid front door, set squarely into its plain front. But the porch was a handsome one and the paint on its window frames was immaculate and a neat border of spring flowers testified to a careful gardener. Alethea beat a tattoo on the door knocker and opened the door, calling out as she went inside, and her grandmother, a brisk upright woman in her late sixties, came from the back of the house to greet her.

Mrs Thomas kissed her granddaughter with pleasure. They were much of a height and her keen eyes stared into Alethea's large brown ones with faint worry in their depths, but she didn't make any remark about Alethea's still too pale face, instead she enquired as to the journey, observed that there was steak and kidney pie for supper and expressed the hope that Alethea was hungry enough to do it justice.

It wasn't until the meal, served by Mrs Thomas's devoted housekeeper, Mrs Bustle, was over and they were sitting round the small log fire in the comfortable, rather shabby sitting room, that Mrs Thomas asked casually: 'You've been busy? You look washed out, Alethea.' She frowned a little. 'I sometimes wish you would give up that job at Theobald's and get something nearer here in a small hospital where the work isn't so exacting.'

Alethea picked a thread off her skirt. 'I enjoy my work, Granny, even when I'm tired, but if you would like me to get something locally, I'll do that.'

Mrs Thomas's frown deepened. 'Indeed you will not, my dear. I wouldn't dream of spoiling a promising career through my selfishness.' She stopped frowning, picked up her knitting and went on in a carefully casual way: 'You have no intention of getting married? You must meet any number of men…'

'Yes, Granny, I do—most of them are married…'

'And those that aren't?'

'Well, I go out sometimes—quite often, but there isn't any particular one.' She added honestly: 'Not now, at any rate.'

Her grandmother nodded, pleased that she had guessed rightly although all she said was: 'There are plenty of other good fish in the sea.' She added gently: 'Do you mind very much, my dear?'

Alethea bent forward to poke the fire. 'Yes, I do, Granny. You see, I thought he was going to marry me…'

'And of course you have to see him every day?'

'Yes.'

'Awkward for you. Could you not take a holiday?'

'And run away, Granny? I can't do that. I—I expect

it won't be so bad in a day or two. One gets over these things.'

Her grandmother opened her mouth to say something and then thought better of it; instead she embarked on a long account of the last WI meeting, of which she was president. It lasted until bedtime.

But if she had hoped that it might take her granddaughter's mind off her unhappiness, she was mistaken. Alethea came down to breakfast the next morning looking as though she had hardly slept a wink, which she hadn't. She had thought that once away from Theobald's with no chance of seeing Nick, she might feel better. Instead, she thought about him all the time, allowing herself to dream foolish little daydreams in which he arrived at her grandmother's door, unable to live without her. Her usually sensible mind rejected this absurdity, but the daydreams persisted, although she did her best to dispel them by a bout of gardening, a walk to the village for the groceries and then a game of chess with her grandmother, who having her wits about her and being good at the game anyway, beat her to a standstill.

She went back on the following evening, sorry to leave the quiet little house which had been her home since her parents had died, but excited at the thought of seeing Nick again.

And she did see him; he was crossing the yard at the back of the hospital where the staff parked their cars. Staff Nurse Petts was with him and they were obviously making for his car. As they drew level with her, Marie Petts accorded her a smug smile. Nick said, 'Good

evening, Sister Thomas,' with the air of only just remembering who she was.

Alethea, rather pale with her desire to fling herself
at Nick, wished them both a serene 'Hullo,' and would
have gone on her way, but Marie wasn't going to be
done out of her triumph. She stopped, so that Nick had
to stop too, and said with false friendliness: 'We're
going to the Palladium—that marvellous show
everyone's talking about.'

Alethea, listening to her own voice, cool and
pleasant, marvelled at it. 'I hear it's quite super…' She
would have babbled on, intent on letting them both see
that she didn't care two straws even though there was
a cold lump of misery under her ribs, but she was interrupted. Mr van Diederijk, sprung apparently from the
ground, so silently had he joined them, spoke before she
could utter any more banalities.

'There you are, Alethea,' he remarked placidly. 'I
was beginning to think that that funny little car of yours
had broken down. Can you manage to change in twenty
minutes or so? I've booked a table for half past eight.'

He had slipped between her and the other two so that
they didn't see her startled face and open mouth. After
a moment she began: 'But I…'

'Need longer? You can have an extra five minutes,
then—I'll wait in the main entrance.'

She turned without a word and almost ran in to the
Nurses' Home entrance, up the stairs and into her room,
where she sat down on the bed without bothering to take
off her jacket. Of course Mr van Diederijk hadn't meant
a word of it. He had rescued her from an awkward

situation, that was all; she would have a bath and go to bed early and thank him for his kindness when she saw him again. She was already in her dressing gown when one of the home maids knocked on the door and told her that she was wanted on the telephone, and just for a second the absurd idea that it might be Nick crossed her mind. It wasn't; Mr van Diederijk's calm voice asked matter-of-factly if she was changing. 'Because if you are, put on something pretty. I thought we might go to Eatons.'

'Oh, I thought—that is, I thought that you were just helping me out, or something.' She added doggedly: 'You were, weren't you? You didn't mean to ask me out to dinner…'

His chuckle was comforting and reassuring. 'Oh, yes, I was helping you out, but I certainly meant to ask you to dine with me, both this evening and as frequently as possible.'

She took the receiver from her ear and looked at it, wondering if she could have heard him aright. After a minute she said: 'Thank you, I'd like to come out this evening. I'll be very quick.'

Something pretty, he had said. She had an almost new crêpe dress, smoky grey delicately patterned with amber and a misty green. She had worn it once to go out with Nick and as she put it on she remembered that he had barely noticed it. She zipped it up defiantly, brushed out her hair so that it curled on her neck, dug her feet into slippers, caught up the dark grey flannel coat she had bought years ago and which was happily dateless and ran downstairs.

Mr van Diederijk was waiting just where he said he would be and she sighed with relief without knowing it. He made some commonplace remark as she joined him, opened the door and led her to the Jaguar and during the brief journey he kept the conversation firmly in his own hands; even if she had wanted to say anything about her meeting with Nick he didn't give her the chance. It was the same during their dinner, a delicious meal—smoked salmon, pork escalope and a rich creamy dessert. They drank Hock, and Alethea, considerably cheered by two glasses of it, prudently refused the brandy offered with her coffee. She was pouring second cups when Mr van Diederijk observed: 'That's a pretty dress,' and then: 'Do you like dancing?'

She remembered the evenings she had gone dancing with Nick. Her 'Yes, I do' was so hesitant that he went on smoothly:

'We must try it one evening, but in the meantime would you come to a theatre with me? Saturday evening, perhaps—there's a play I rather wanted to see, I think you might enjoy it too.'

She didn't say anything for a few minutes and then she asked a question. 'Why are you being so very kind? I mean, asking me out to dinner—twice within days and then pretending that we were spending the evening together…'

'Well, we are, aren't we? Spending the evening together.' His voice was bland. 'And I'm not being kind, Alethea, rather should I say that I like to see fair play, and it seems to me that young Penrose isn't playing fair.' He looked at her thoughtfully, frowning a little. 'If you want him back you must put on a bold front.'

'I don't want him back,' she uttered the lie so hotly that it was quite apparent that there wasn't a word of truth in it, 'and what's more, I can't see that it's any business of yours, Mr van Diederijk.'

'You are of course quite right. I apologise.' He added coolly: 'I expect you would like to go.' He lifted a finger and took the bill and signed it, and Alethea cried sharply: 'Oh, I quite forgot—I still owe you for the other night...'

She was stopped by the look of distaste on her companion's face. 'Allow me to settle that with Penrose,' he said blandly. There was nothing for her to do but get up and go. She did it with outward calm, smarting from his polite snub, and engaged him in a trivial conversation all the way back to Theobald's, where she thanked him with the nice manners of a small girl who had been well drilled in the social niceties.

Mr van Diederijk listened to her, his head a little on one side. When she had finished, all he said was: 'Not a successful evening, but there will be others.'

This remark sent her crossly to her bed; there would be no more evenings, she decided, and then remembered that she had said that she would go to the theatre with him. Oh well, she conceded, just that once more, and then never again.

In view of this resolution it was upsetting to receive a brief note from him on the following day, telling her that he had been called back to Holland, and must regretfully postpone their date. She stuck it back in its envelope and left it on the desk in her office, and presently when she went back there with Sir Walter and Nick, she saw him looking at it. She picked it up and put it in her pocket without a word and had the satisfaction of hearing Nick ask Sir Walter if Mr van Diederijk would be operating on the case they had been looking at.

'Back in Holland,' mumbled Sir Walter through a mouthful of biscuit, 'had an emergency call from his brother. He'll be back, though. I want to get his opinion on that leg we've been looking at.'

He launched into technicalities and Alethea poured his second cup of coffee and listened with one ear, while she speculated as to whether Mr van Diederijk would ask her out again. It was difficult to keep her mind on this, because Nick was sitting close to her and she was only too well aware of him. He was still behaving as though she was someone he had only just met and didn't like, anyway, and she was hard put to it to maintain a serene front. She still felt terrible about him, but pride forbade her to show her feelings and there was a certain sad satisfaction in knowing that she was being successful in this. She saw the two men out of the ward presently and went back to her ward round which they had interrupted.

Saturday came and went, and it was lucky that she was so very busy, she told herself, for now that she had no date, she was under no obligation to go off duty punctually on Saturday evening—indeed, she stayed on for an hour or more, much to Sue's surprise and faint annoyance; surely Sister Thomas knew her well enough by now to know that she could safely leave the patients to her without fussing round in a totally untypical manner? It came to her presently that it might be on account of Nick Penrose. Alethea had said nothing and her manner towards him had given nothing away, all the same… Sue nodded her head wisely and when Alethea at last went off duty, wished her good night with genuine sympathy.

Sunday and Monday were surprisingly quiet and Alethea had given herself her days off on Tuesday and Wednesday that week. Thursday was to be a heavy operating day, and she liked to be on duty for theatre days, anyway. She went home on Monday evening, driving through the lovely April evening and seeing nothing of it, her mind busy. She would waste no more time in being sorry for herself, but she knew that she would have to get away from Nick before she could take up the threads of her life once more. She would have liked to have given in her notice there and then, but that wasn't possible; she would have to work her month out, like everyone else, and find herself another job. It might look as though she were running away from an unpleasant situation, and in a way, she was and probably Nick would get some satisfaction from it, but her friends would understand and as far as she could see, it was the best way, indeed, the only way.

She told her grandmother of her vague plans that evening and that lady, without asking any awkward questions, heartily agreed with her before embarking on a series of helpful suggestions as to where she should go.

'Give London a rest,' she urged. 'Why not

Edinburgh? I know it's a long way and you won't get home nearly as often, but you'll be breaking new ground.' Mrs Thomas settled back in her chair. 'Get out that port the vicar gave me at Christmas, child, we'll have a glass while we're thinking.'

But there was nothing much to discuss, when all was said and done. Alethea loved her grandmother dearly, but she had no intention of burdening her with her troubles; all the same, it was pleasant to sit there and make plans for the future with someone who really was interested. It was probably the port which made her sleep soundly for the first time in nights.

She awoke early to a splendid morning with a brisk wind and sunshine, which, while not over-warm, gave promise of a lovely day. She lay in bed for a little while and then remembered how Mrs Bustle had been grumbling mildly about the spring cleaning, something which she insisted upon doing each year. Alethea got out of bed, got into slacks and a thin sweater and crept downstairs. The sitting room curtains, Mrs Bustle had observed gloomily, simply had to come down and have a good blow.

Alethea made tea, drank it at the open kitchen door, gave Podge the cat his morning milk and set about getting the curtains out into the garden. They were old and faded, but their damask was still good. They were also very heavy; she hauled them down the garden path to the very end where the clothes line was, and hung them upon it, and then, quite carried away by her success, went into the dining room and did the same for the green serge hanging at the big sash window there.

She would make more tea, she decided, and take a cup upstairs to both ladies before getting the breakfast; Mrs Bustle could do with an extra hour in bed. The old ladies were grateful. With strict instructions about breakfast she was allowed to go downstairs again, lay the table and put on the porridge. She was hungry by now and the packet of Rice Crispies she found in a cupboard was welcome; she sat on the kitchen table, eating them, her head, just for the moment, happily free of unhappy thoughts.

'Now that's what I like to see,' said Mr van Diederijk cheerfully from the window behind her, 'a strong young woman working in the kitchen.'

She turned to look at him, surprised at the little rush of pleasure she felt at the sight of him. She answered him through a mouthful of crispies: 'I very much doubt if you ever bother to go to the kitchen, whether there's a strong young woman there or not.' She frowned a little; such a description made her feel large and muscley.

'Oh, but I do—I have a housekeeper, a Scotswoman who bakes Dundee cakes for me. I'm partial to a nice Dundee cake. May I come in?'

And when she nodded he lifted a long leg over the sill and slid neatly into the room. He was looking very trendy, she considered. Not young any more but distinguished, and his clothes were just right.

He put out a hand and she shook some Rice Crispies into it. 'You pay your visits very early,' she observed.

'I came over on the Harwich ferry, it got in just after six.' He glanced at his watch. 'It's almost eight o'clock. Have you had breakfast?'

'Not yet. Would you like some? My grandmother and Mrs Bustle will be down very soon, I'm waiting for them.' She got down off the table. 'How did you know I was here, or did you just happen to be passing?'

He looked vague. 'Oh, someone or other told me where you lived and I thought that if I called about breakfast time…'

Alethea laughed and at the same time felt vaguely peeved that he hadn't come specially to see her, only on the offchance of getting breakfast. She thrust the thought aside as absurd; now if it had been Nick…

'Don't look so sad.' Mr van Diederijk's voice was kind. 'I'm not young Penrose, but at least I provide you with company.'

She lifted startled eyes to his. 'However did you know that I was thinking that?'

'Logic.' He wandered over to the open door. 'What a charming garden. Why are all the curtains hanging on the line and not at the windows?'

Alethea explained, and halfway through Mrs Bustle came in, was introduced, declared herself pleased to meet their visitor, enquired if he liked two eggs with his bacon or three and ordered them with brisk kindness out of her kitchen. 'The sitting room's got the sun,' she pointed out, 'though it looks a bit bare without those curtains, and as for you, Miss Alethea, you'd do well to go and wash your face and hands and comb your hair for your breakfast.'

'The worst of these old family servants and friends,' remarked Mr van Diederijk, ushered into the sitting room by Alethea, 'is that having known you since you were so high, they never allow you to grow up. I know—I've one at home.'

'The one who bakes the cakes?'

'The very same. Are you on duty tomorrow?'

She paused at the door. 'Yes—I drove down.'

'Ah, well—I'll drive you back. You can always come down by train and drive back next time?'

'Well, yes, I could. But I'm not going until this evening.'

'Ah—I'm invited to spend the day?' His voice was bland. 'I shall enjoy that. Besides, I can hang those curtains for you.'

Alethea was much struck, when at the end of the day she was sitting beside Mr van Diederijk on their way back to Theobald's, at the pleasant time she—indeed all of them—had had. Her grandmother had liked him and had spent quite some time in conversation with him while Alethea and Mrs Bustle got lunch, and as for the housekeeper, he was an instant success, and although he didn't get Dundee cake for his tea, he certainly had his appetite coaxed with feather-light sponges, home-made scones and Mrs Bustle's own jam. And when they left she was surprised at her grandmother's sincere wish that he should call again. And he had agreed to do so, too.

'It was rather a quiet day for you,' she ventured as he sent the Jaguar racing ahead.

'I like quiet days. What gave you the idea that I didn't?' he wanted to know.

'Nothing—only you live in London and I expect you go out a good deal.'

'I live in Groningen, too, and I like nothing better

than to be at home.' He overtook the cars ahead of him and steadied the car's pace. 'And you?' He glanced at her. 'Your grandmother tells me that you're thinking of leaving Theobald's. A good idea, but of course you can only leave for one reason.'

She turned to look at him. 'What do you mean?'

'Be bright, dear girl. If you leave to go to another job, your Nick is going to hear of it and he'll know you're running away. If you leave, it must be to get married.'

Alethea sat up, scattering her handbag and its contents all over the floor. 'There, look what you've made me do!' she declared unfairly.

'We'll pick everything up presently. Did you hear what I said, Alethea?'

'Yes—but how can I do that? I don't know anyone— and besides, I don't want to get married.' She swallowed. 'Well, you know what I mean, only if it's Nick.' She added crossly: 'And I don't know why I talk to you like this.'

He ignored everything she had said. 'We'll have to see,' was all he said, and he went on to talk about the morrow's work. He was, she decided, very annoying at times, pretending not to hear, probably not listening. She wished him a rather snappy goodnight and was rendered speechless when he suddenly pulled her close and kissed her. When she had her breath back she demanded indignantly: 'What was that for?'

'A matter of expediency—your Nick came into the hall and it seemed a good idea to give him something to think about. There's nothing like a little competition.'

'Thank you,' said Alethea. Young men usually kissed

her because they wanted to, Mr van Diederijk apparently did it by way of necessity; she wasn't sure if she minded or not. She wished him goodnight for a second time and went to her room. She had hoped to see Nick as she went, but there was no sign of him. Surely if he had any feeling left for her at all he would have wanted to know why Mr van Diederijk had kissed her? She sighed; she was wasting time, her pride told her, and the sooner she left the better. 'But I'll not get married,' she told herself out loud.

CHAPTER THREE

SHE WAS OF THE same mind the next morning and indeed she was of a mind to tell Mr van Diederijk this if she had the opportunity. But there was no chance to speak to him. True, he paid a fleeting visit to the ward, elegant and rather awe-inspiring in his dark grey suiting and expensive tie, but he was very much the consultant; beyond wishing him a pleasant good morning, proffering the notes of the case which he wished to see and escorting him to the ward door with an equally pleasant goodbye, Alethea prudently said nothing. Probably he would come again, when there might be a few minutes in which to tell him that she had no intention of even considering his ridiculous suggestion. What did it matter what Nick thought, anyway? she asked herself as she penned instructions in the day book. It was galling to discover much later in the day, that he had been back while she had been down in X-Ray, speaking her mind about some missing films urgently needed on the ward. What was more, he had stopped to chat to Sue. 'Almost ten minutes,' declared that young lady. 'Anyone would think that he hadn't anything else in the world to do, and when I asked him if he wanted to see you all he said was: "I think not, Staff, not for the moment."' She sighed. 'He's very good-looking and his eyes twinkle.'

'Pooh!' exclaimed Alethea, suddenly cross for no reason, and then to cover up her little outburst: 'X-Ray say they haven't a clue where those films are, they say they gave them to Nurse Jenkins, although no one remembers actually doing that. I'll have a word with her, I think.' She wrinkled her pretty forehead. 'What a waste of time when there's so much to be done!'

And it wasn't just the lost films, the whole day had been a series of small hold-ups, misunderstandings and delays. Alethea went off duty finally, glad that it was over. It wasn't until she was in bed that she remembered that she had meant to go and see the Principal Nursing Officer about leaving. 'Tomorrow,' she told herself, and resolutely shut her eyes, but before she went to sleep she found herself remembering very clearly what good company Mr van Diederijk had been at her home, sitting opposite her at her grandmother's table, tucking into Mrs Bustle's steak and kidney pie with relish. He grew on one, she decided, and slept.

As so often happened, the next morning went as smoothly as the previous one had gone consistently wrong. Enough staff for once, all the operation cases of the day before doing exactly as they should, even the missing X-Ray films turning up. Alethea, her round done and the wheels of morning work turning smoothly, retired to her office to tackle the off-duty book, fill in the requisitions, make diplomatic telephone calls to the laundry, the dietitian and the Social Worker and presently, to enjoy a cup of coffee with Sue.

She was deep in the off-duty when the door opened and without lifting her head she said: 'Sue, I want Mr Brook's leg up a bit…' and when no one answered she looked up.

'Good morning,' observed Mr van Diederijk. 'Your staff nurse assures me that you are more or less free for a little while. I should like to talk to you.'

She put down her pen. 'Now?'

'Now. About Penrose.' He lifted a large hand as she began to protest and went on in a matter-of-fact voice: 'He is the only man you have loved.' It wasn't a question, just a statement of fact.

Alethea went pink and said 'Yes,' gruffly.

'You weren't having an affair, of course.'

The pink flamed to red and she choked a little. 'Certainly not!'

'Forgive me, I don't know why I asked that question; it was quite unnecessary. I wonder, would you consider marrying me, Alethea?'

Indignation and surprise turned to sheer amazement.

'Will I what?' she repeated slowly.

'Consider marrying me.' He was as much at his ease as he might have been asking her if she had an empty bed on the ward.

She rearranged everything on her desk, trying to think what to say, and when nothing came, she rearranged everything again.

'Let us review the situation calmly,' suggested Mr van Diederijk in an unhurried fashion. 'You wish to run away from a situation which is no longer tolerable to you, but you haven't quite enough courage to do so.' And when she jerked her head up: 'No, don't interrupt. You would like a way out, wouldn't you, for to remain here has become untenable, hasn't it? But your pride must be kept intact at all costs, your reason for leaving must have nothing to suggest that you are running away. I offer you a means to that end. No, allow me to finish. I need a wife, or more accurately, my home needs a mistress, and I need someone to entertain my friends and provide a secure background for my children.' He paused and held her astonished gaze with calm blue eyes. 'Oh, yes, I have been married. My wife and I were divorced by mutual consent ten years ago. She is married to some rich South American and lives in Brazil—or is it Peru? I can never remember. She has no interest in the children—twins, a boy, Sarel, and a girl, Jacomina. They are eleven years old.'

Alethea asked breathlessly: 'She left them when they were a year old? She couldn't…'

'She could and she did. They need a mother very badly, Alethea, but I must make it quite clear that I do not need a wife.'

She pushed a tidy pile of papers away so roughly that they fell in a hopeless muddle to the floor. 'You could get yourself a housekeeper.' She remembered as she said it that he already had one. 'Or a nursemaid,' she added.

He was quite unruffled. 'I already have both. My housekeeper I mentioned, she is elderly and excellent, but bringing up children is not part of her work. The nursemaid has been with the children since they were babies. She loves them dearly, spoils them utterly and can no longer cope. They need kind authority, understanding and someone to confide in and love.'

'Why not you?' Her voice was a little sharp.

'I am not a woman. I love them, make no mistake about that, but there are so many things I cannot do or say which a woman—a mother—can.'

Alethea opened her mouth ready to utter the telling remarks she had a mind to utter, but she had no chance. The door opened again and Sue came in, hesitated, said: 'I'll bring in the coffee, shall I? You too, sir?' and retreated.

'I...' began Alethea, and was interrupted once more, this time by one of the nurses, who asked in a scared voice if she could go to coffee and then turned and ran, and this time Mr van Diederijk leaned one vast shoulder against the door jamb. 'I'll leave you to think it over,' he said placidly. 'There are no strings attached, my dear. As I said, I don't want a wife, I've had my fill of loving,' his placid voice was suddenly bitter, 'and that I think will suit you. I shall enjoy your companionship and be proud to have you at my table...'

He was at the door when she cried: 'But it's so drastic!'

'Yes? But surely better than staying here for ever, eating your heart out while you preserve an indifference torn in shreds each time you meet Penrose. And you meet half a dozen times a day, do you not?'

He didn't wait for her to answer, but went away, shutting the door very quietly behind him. Alethea sat very still after he had gone, staring down at her folded hands. She was still staring at them when Sue came in with the coffee tray.

'You look as though someone has hit you on the head with a hammer,' observed that young lady. She looked a little anxiously at Alethea. 'I say, nothing's wrong, is it? I mean, on the ward?'

'No—everything's fine.' Alethea summoned up a smile. 'It wasn't anything to do with the ward.' And Sue forbore from asking any more questions. Sister Thomas was a poppet, but she had an air of reserve, even with those with whom she worked, which prevented prying, and when she broached the subject of the new batch of student nurses expected on the ward the next day, Sue followed her lead and they talked of nothing else.

Alethea got through her busy day, plagued by the tiresome thought that Mr van Diederijk had left her to think his preposterous idea over and hadn't said more than that. How long would it be before he turned up again, wanting to know her answer? And did he imagine that it was something she could make up her mind about in an hour or so? Not, she reminded herself peevishly, that she had any intention of even considering such a ridiculous suggestion. She proceeded to consider it for the rest of the day and far into the night and at last fell asleep, declaring that he was either mad or playing some trick upon her. She was aware as she closed her eyes that neither of these suppositions held an atom of truth.

It seemed that Mr van Diederijk's idea of leaving her to think it over was a timeless one; she saw nothing of him for the rest of that week, at the end of which she flounced off to her grandmother's for her days off in a quite nasty temper so that Mrs Bustle took her severely to task for glowering at her and taking no interest in the rhubarb jam-making, declaring that such tantrums belonged to childhood when they would have been suitably punished. And as for Mrs Thomas, she waited patiently for her granddaughter to tell her whatever was on her mind and causing her to be so unlike her usual serene self. And sure enough, when Alethea returned from shopping in the village and found that Mr van Diederijk had telephoned to say that he would be down to drive her back after lunch the next day, she could contain herself no longer; she dumped her basket on the kitchen table and went in search of her grandparent.

Mrs Thomas was sitting in the back porch, knitting, but she put it down as Alethea joined her and said: 'Yes dear?' in an inviting voice.

'Granny,' began Alethea, 'I want to talk to you…'

'Yes, my dear, I thought perhaps you did. It's about Mr van Diederijk, I take it?'

'How did you know? I've never said…'

Mrs Thomas looked smug. 'Exactly, Alethea. You have my full attention.'

Her grandmother heard her out without interruption. Only when Alethea had come to an end did she say: 'I'm sorry, darling,' and then: 'You like Mr van Diederijk?'

Alethea examined her well-kept hands at some length, frowning fiercely, and muttered: 'Yes.'

'And you are sure in your heart that this—Nick does not love you?'

'Oh, yes. I'm sure of that, Granny.' Her voice was steady, but try as she might she couldn't keep the bitterness out of it.

'You must decide for yourself, Alethea, you know that, don't you?' She paused. 'He will expect an answer tomorrow.'

'Probably he will, but since he merely told me that he would leave me to think it over, I don't see why he should expect an answer just when he wants it.' She added loftily: 'After all, it was rather like a business deal.'

Her grandmother eyed her thoughtfully. 'Well, my dear, it is just that, is it not? And one which could benefit you both,' she added matter-of-factly. 'Companionship in marriage is important, you know, so is mutual respect and liking. It is possible to love someone without any of these things, even to dislike them.'

And that's how I feel about Nick, thought Alethea unhappily, for I don't like him, only I can't forget him…

Her grandmother went on, apparently talking to herself: 'Love, if there is nothing else with it, can be utterly destroyed and leave nothing in its place, but liking and respect can grow into deep affection and even love.'

'You want me to marry Mr van Diederijk,' said Alethea baldly.

'I have already told you, darling, you must decide for yourself.' Mrs Thomas paused. 'Don't say anything now, child—whatever you do decide is your concern and his. How old is he, by the way?'

'I don't know, Granny, but if his children are eleven

years old be must be in his late thirties—he looks older than that.'

'And you are twenty-seven,' her grandmother reminded her.

Alethea nodded. 'Getting long in the tooth…'

'But don't let that be a reason for marrying, my dear.'

'Oh, I can promise you that—if I did decide to marry him, and that's very unlikely, it would be because of Nick. Nothing really matters any more, Granny—I shall forget him in time, shan't I? But will it be quite fair?'

Her grandmother forbore from pointing out that if she had no intention of marrying Mr van Diederijk the question wouldn't arise. 'Quite fair,' she observed firmly, 'because he knows everything there is to know about it.'

Alethea said: 'Well, yes…' in a vague fashion and presently wandered off to lay the table for lunch. The matter wasn't discussed again that day and Alethea didn't allow herself to think about it either; she knew that this was a silly thing to do because on the next day she would have to give Mr van Diederijk his answer, but since, as she told herself far more frequently than she realised, she was going to refuse him in any case, there was no point in teasing her already muddled head. All the same, she slept badly and when she wakened after a bad night, her determination was all the stronger. It was a pity that she couldn't justify her resolution for doing so, especially as the alternative was hardly a pleasant prospect; all the same, she made up her lovely face with more than usual care and arranged her hair with an eye as to its most becoming appearance. True,

Mr van Diederijk wasn't coming until the afternoon, and that would probably mean teatime, but there was no harm in being prepared. Besides, she would have ample time in which to refurbish her person before then.

She was wrong. She was wiping the dishes Mrs Bustle was washing after their lunch when his vast form blocked the kitchen doorway.

His, 'Hullo, Mrs Thomas told me to come in this way,' was genial without showing any undue eagerness and Alethea was instantly annoyed; there he was, elegant in his casual country clothes, worn with such an air, while she was only too aware that her nose was shining and her carefully arranged hair had come loose in curly tendrils. Why couldn't Granny have told him to ring the front door bell or even got out of her garden chair and brought him in the right way and not through the kitchen door; it would have given her time to run a comb through her hair…

Her 'Hullo,' was almost drowned by Mrs Bustle's anxious voice wanting to know if he had had his lunch, and at his quick, 'Yes, thanks,' Alethea guessed that he hadn't; after all, it was only a little after half past one…

'Have you come straight from Theobald's?' she asked.

He nodded. 'A busy morning—I'm afraid we've filled your ward up for you once more.'

She polished a spoon with care. 'So you had no time for lunch, did you?'

His eyes met hers across the pleasant, rather cluttered kitchen. He said simply: 'I wanted to see you, Alethea.'

She blinked with surprise and pinkened a little. 'Would sandwiches and coffee do? or beer?'

He smiled then, a friendly grin which she found herself answering. 'Beer, please. And I would love a sandwich.'

Mrs Bustle snorted her concern. 'You get the beer, Miss Alethea, and go into the garden. I'll be out in a brace of shakes with something tasty.'

Alethea got the beer and took her companion into the garden where Mrs Thomas was quite obviously waiting for them. 'Come here and sit down,' she called. 'Such a lovely day, and you must forgive an old woman for being lazy.'

She then proceeded to engage him in a conversation which while not exactly excluding Alethea, certainly didn't give her any chance to say much for herself, and when presently Mrs Bustle came with a tray loaded with sandwiches, one or two of her own pork pies, and a slice of rhubarb pie, well sugared, and arranged this repast on a small table at Mr van Diederijk's elbow, conversation was kept to a polite minimum while he demolished these dainties.

He sat back at length. 'You are a magnificent cook, Mrs Bustle,' he observed to that lady, who had pounced out upon them several times to make sure that he was eating his fill. He turned to Mrs Thomas. 'And you, Mrs Thomas, are a delightful hostess. Thank you both.'

He didn't say anything to Alethea, which considering she had done very little to entertain him was natural enough—indeed, except for the odd remark during the next half an hour, he had very little to say to her. But presently Mrs Thomas observed: 'I shall now take a nap. We will have tea at four o'clock, Alethea—out here, I think. Take Sarre for a walk.'

If Alethea had been an ill-natured girl, she would have muttered her annoyance. As it was she said politely, 'Very well, Granny, although perhaps Mr van Diederijk would like a rest too…' She stopped there because she could see that he was laughing silently at her, but all he said was: 'Sarre, if you could remember. I don't feel quite so old then.'

They had taken a few steps when Mrs Thomas asked: 'If I am not being impertinent, Sarre, how old are you?'

'Thirty-nine, Mrs Thomas, and sometimes I feel twice that age.'

'And sometimes you look the half of it.' She closed her eyes with a loud sigh. 'Now run along—when you reach my age it doesn't matter whether you look young or old; you need a nap after lunch.'

They laughed gently at her because she expected them to and then started off down the path which led round the rambling little house and down the garden at the back to where a gate opened on to a narrow rutted lane. Here Alethea paused and glanced at her companion's expensive, well-polished shoes. 'It's rather rough,' she began, and then with sudden vexation: 'I wanted to tidy my hair…'

'It looks perfectly all right,' said Mr van Diederijk in a soothing voice, 'and that is only because you are trying to put off the inevitable.'

Alethea stared silently at him. It was perfectly true, but when it was voiced out loud in that matter-of-fact way, it sounded a bit silly. He opened the gate and stood aside while she went through. 'I've come for my answer, Alethea.' He closed the gate. 'Which is it to be, yes or no?'

He showed no impatience when she didn't answer but strolled along beside her, a man to all appearances content with his world. She peeped at his profile—and a handsome one it was too, she had to admit, with its high-bridged nose and firm mouth and chin. He caught her looking before she could turn away, his blue eyes compelling her to speak.

To her utter astonishment she said 'Yes,' when all the time she had intended to say no, and still feeling most strangely that the words were being put into her mouth: 'At least, I think so.'

His smile was so kind and understanding that she smiled too.

'It was a difficult decision for you to make,' he observed, 'but I think it is the right one and it goes without saying that I am delighted.' He took her hand and stood looking down at her thoughtfully. 'I believe that we shall get on extremely well together. All the same, I'll not hurry you—if you want more time to think it over...?' His raised brows emphasised the question so that she said: 'No—no, I don't,' not giving herself time to consider the matter. All the same she felt relief when he went on easily: 'Shall we make a bargain? If at any time during our engagement you feel you don't want to marry me after all, will you tell me?'

She returned his look with wide-eyed honesty. 'Yes, I promise that, but I don't change my mind, you know.'

'Good. Would you consent to a short engagement? A month—six weeks? During that time I'll take you over to Holland so that you can meet the children and some of my family. You would like to marry here, I expect?'

She thought about it. 'Yes, please and very quietly. Can—may you marry in church? I mean…you're divorced…'

'There are, I believe, clergy who will marry a divorced person even though it isn't the usual rule. What about your local vicar?'

'We could ask. Isn't there a Service of Blessing we could have if we have to go to a registrar's office?'

'So I've heard. Shall I find out and let you know?'

'Please. I'll have to give in my notice.'

'Tomorrow morning if you could manage that. Must it be a month?'

They were strolling along now, the sun warm on them and a nice little breeze blowing Alethea's already untidy hair into still more curls.

'Well, I have two weeks' holiday due, which means that I could leave in a fortnight…'

'Will you arrange that? I shall be at Theobald's for the next week, then I have to go back to Holland for a few days. I'll come over for you when you're free and you can spend a week there and then return here and I'll come over for the wedding. Would that suit you?'

He seemed to have it all planned very nicely. Just for a second she wondered if it would have been like that if it was Nick she were marrying and not this quiet, persistent man beside her. He was being very businesslike about it, but then did she want it otherwise? She sighed without knowing it and he said: 'Don't allow your thoughts to wander, Alethea, regretting the past will make it harder to bear.'

He stopped again and took her gently by the shoulders and turned her round to face him. 'Could you turn the page?' he asked softly. 'It needs courage, but it can be done.' He bent and kissed her lightly on her cheek. 'There's a seal on our friendship.'

Alethea studied him at length. 'You're a very nice person,' she told him. 'You're sure about it? I mean, you're not getting much of a bargain.'

'I hardly think of you as a bargain, my dear; rest assured that I am getting exactly what I want. And now shall I tell you something of my home?'

It was in Groningen, he told her, in the very heart of the city, and Alethea instantly conjured up a picture of a red brick town house with square bay windows and ugly plaster work adding an unnecessary decoration.

'There's a garden,' went on Sarre, 'not a large one, though, and a shed or two. The housekeeper and Nanny you know about already, they're helped by Juffrouw Bril who comes each morning and Nel, who lives in, lastly Al who turns his hand to anything. Then the children, Sarel and Jacomina, they have their own rooms of course and a playroom, but they eat their meals with me and we spend as much time together as I can manage. Oh, and there is my dog, Rough, the children's puppy, Nero, a couple of cats and a selection of mice, gerbils and Sarel's white rat.'

Alethea shuddered inwardly at the idea of the rat but managed a cheerful: 'Quite a houseful!'

'Yes. I'm away from time to time—sometimes for several days. I hope that you will be able to come with me occasionally.'

'That will be nice. Have you any family?'

'My mother and father are in New Zealand, visiting my young sister. She's married to a civil engineer who's on a job there for a year or so.' He added: 'I have a grandfather, too, a wonderful old man; he always says exactly what he thinks regardless of the circumstances. And I have a brother, younger than I—Wienand, he's not married, he lives in Groningen too, he has a big practice and we work closely together. He is a leading osteopath; we find that we get splendid results. I think you will like him.'

Alethea said soberly: 'I expect I shall. I'm a little nervous of meeting Sarel and Jacomina...'

'No need. I'm sure they'll be delighted to have such a young and beautiful mother.'

'Yes? But I'm not their mother, Sarre.'

'They have never known her,' his voice was harsh, 'they believe that she died when they were babies. When they are a little older I shall explain to them, but at present it would be cruel.'

Greatly daring, Alethea asked: 'Did you love her very much?'

He didn't answer her. 'Perhaps we should be getting back,' he said smoothly. 'Your grandmother said four o'clock, did she not? Would you be ready to leave directly after tea?'

So she was to marry him, thought Alethea, but she wasn't going to be allowed to share his life, not that part of it, at any rate. She didn't mind, she decided, his past was his own concern and indeed she wasn't interested in it. Now if it had been Nick... Her thoughts were interrupted by her companion's voice, wanting to know if she would prefer to fly over to Holland or go by sea.

She wrenched her thoughts back to the present. 'Oh, I don't think I mind, I've never flown; if Granny and I have gone away on holiday we've always gone somewhere like Scotland or Wales or the West Country.'

'Then we'll fly, it's very quick and I'll arrange for Al to fetch us from Schipol.'

'Al?'

'I told you about him. He's my manservant; he—er—joined us ten years ago and is a devoted friend as well as a splendid worker.'

'Oh—what does he do, exactly?'

Sarre laughed. 'Everything and anything that he wants to do. And when I'm away he keeps an eye on the children, manages the finances, mends fuses, baths the dogs, takes the children out for the day if they're free. I should be lost without him.'

'You have a lot of people in your house, Sarre.' Alethea spoke doubtfully and wished she knew more about her companion.

'It must seem so, but if you count them up, they're mostly children and animals.' Which was true enough, she supposed.

Mrs Thomas was awake and waiting for them. 'A pleasant walk, my dears?' she wanted to know, and beamed at them, looking as near smug as an elderly lady of her sort could.

It was Sarre who answered her. 'Very pleasant,' he agreed. 'The country around here is delightful. Mrs Thomas, Alethea has agreed to marry me. I hope that you are pleased.'

'I'm delighted.' She beamed at them both. 'I'll wish you very happy. When will you marry?'

Alethea had to laugh. 'Granny, we're only just engaged! But we thought in about six weeks' time.'

'I never did agree with long engagements. I met your grandfather at a Christmas party and we married on New Year's Day.' She sighed. 'And very happy we were, too. As you will be. Come and give me a kiss, Alethea.'

Tea was a gay meal, with Mrs Bustle sharing it with them so that she could hear the exciting news while she plied Mr van Diederijk with scones and cake and the little biscuits which were her particular forte, but it was she and Mrs Thomas who did most of the talking. Sarre seemed content to sit back and allow the conversation to flow back and forth, joining in in his pleasant calm voice from time to time, while Alethea was almost totally silent. She had said that she would marry him and burnt her boats behind her, now she was beset with any number of doubts. Supposing Nick wanted to marry her after all? Supposing he asked her not to leave, to make it up and go on as before? Probably it would never be the same again, but all the same...

She bade her grandmother and Mrs Bustle goodbye with her usual serenity, however, and got into the car beside Sarre with every appearance of feeling completely content with her future, so it was a little disconcerting when he observed: 'I asked you to turn the page, Alethea, I meant forwards, not back; it will serve no good purpose brooding over what might have been.'

She coloured faintly. 'Oh—I didn't know, that is, it's hard not to remember—I didn't know it…that you could see…'

He answered this incoherent remark with a wry smile. 'It was so very plain on your face, my dear. Luckily your grandmother and Mrs Bustle were so busily engaged in your wedding clothes and whether to have almond paste on the cake that they didn't notice.'

She turned to look at him. 'Are you sure it will be all right? I will try, I promise you, but just to forget, like that…I don't think I'm very good at it.'

'It gets easier with practice,' said Sarre dryly. 'We'll stop for dinner, shall we? There's a good place at Backhurst Mill.'

They dined unhurriedly and Alethea found herself relaxing under her companion's gentle flow of small talk. The food was good and she found that she had quite an appetite after all, and when Sarre remarked: 'I shall be operating in the morning, shall I see you?' she answered readily that she hoped so, aware that she really meant it.

Sarre made no effort to hurry back. They reached the hospital shortly before midnight and even then they stood talking for a few minutes in its entrance.

'Thank you for my dinner and bringing me back,' Alethea said politely, and then felt foolish at his:

'I hardly think that you need to thank me, my dear. Such small services will be my privilege in the future.'

'Oh, yes, of course.' She smiled a little shyly at him, and then in a burst of confidence added: 'You know, when I got up this morning I'd made up my mind to say no.'

'And what made you change your mind?' he wanted to know quietly.

'I haven't the faintest idea.' She smiled a little. 'But I won't change it again.'

He took her hand and then bent his head and kissed her, a quick light kiss which although it had meant nothing at all, stayed in her mind long after she had wished him goodnight and gone to her bed.

CHAPTER FOUR

THE DAY WAS well advanced before Alethea saw Sarre; she had sent a shattered leg to theatre, followed by a complicated fracture of the scapula and having supervised their safe return to their beds, had gone to her office to sort out the notes, fill in charts and catch up on the morning's work. She was hot and a little untidy, for it was a warm morning and she hadn't paused since she had gone on duty at eight o'clock. She was also hungry and thirsty, for her dinner time had passed, and she saw no chance of going down to the dining room. Mary would make her a pot of tea and a sandwich presently and she could finish her writing while she took these homely refreshments, before going back on to the ward.

She was deciphering Sir Walter's notes, written in a spidery hand, when the door opened and Sarre walked in. He wasted no time in observing that she was busy but plunged at once into instructions about the shattered leg he had restored more or less to its original form that morning; only when he had finished did he ask: 'You've been to your lunch?' and when she said that no, she hadn't, added: 'In that case could your estimable maid bring us a pot of tea? Just while I explain the treatment for that shoulder.'

The tea came, sandwiches too, and Alethea pouring it, remarked: 'You've missed your lunch too, haven't you?' She smiled at him and pushed her cap back a bit so that the curls escaped. 'Share these, I'll not have time to eat them all, anyway.' She took a bite, surprised to find that she felt perfectly at ease with him, glad in fact that he was there. She was pouring second cups when the door opened again and Nick came in. He stopped short when he saw Mr van Diederijk and the scowl on his good-looking face deepened. Before he could say anything Sarre spoke. 'We're going over that case—the scapula, I'd like him on antibiotics for a few days, to be on the safe side. I have written it up.' He lifted an eyebrow. 'Did you want to see Sister about one of the patients? Am I in the way?'

Alethea had gone a little pale, but she finished pouring the tea and handed Sarre's cup to him. She didn't want to be left alone with Nick, and a second later she realised that she need not have worried about that. He had no reasonable excuse to speak to her alone; Sarre was very much his senior and besides, he was no stranger to the ward. For the moment he was working with Sir Walter and was as concerned with the patients as Nick.

All the same she let out a small relieved breath when Nick said sulkily: 'It wasn't anything important, sir, only some notes…I'll come back later.'

He had barely closed the door behind him when Sarre asked: 'Are you off duty this evening, Alethea?'

She nodded. 'But I'll be late. Staff's on, but we're a bit behind with the work and I'll have to stay…'

'You went to see about leaving this morning?'

'Yes—that's settled, I'm to leave in two weeks' time.' She raised her lovely eyes to his. 'Is that OK?'

'Indeed it is. Would you be too tired to come out this evening? Would eight o'clock be too early?'

'I'd like to, thank you,' she said rather formally, 'that should give me plenty of time.'

He went away soon afterwards and she plunged back into the round of chores waiting to be done in the ward. They were always so short of staff, she thought worriedly as she added another weight to yet another leg extended on its Balkan Beam. The Principal Nursing Officer hadn't been too pleased with her that morning. 'When the ward is so busy, Sister,' she had complained, 'surely you could wait a few months—after all, you haven't known Mr van Diederijk very long, have you?'

It hardly seemed worth while pointing out to Miss Gibbs, fifty if she was a day and a born spinster, that it made very little difference whether you knew someone a long time or not—she and Nick had fallen in love within a few minutes of meeting each other. 'Mr van Diederijk's work has to be considered,' she pointed out with becoming meekness, and Miss Gibbs had to concede the point. But grudgingly. Just as grudgingly she had wished Alethea a happy future, her tone implying that the possibility was an unlikely one.

The day wore on. A motorbike accident came in followed by an elderly man who had fallen off a ladder. Alethea counted herself lucky to get away by seven o'clock, and by then she was so tired she wanted nothing but a strong cup of tea and her bed, something which Mr van Diederijk must have guessed at because no sooner had she reached the Home than she was called to the telephone. 'You're tired,' said Sarre's quiet voice in her ear. 'Put on a pretty dress as quickly as you can; I know of a little restaurant where you can doze off between the courses if you want to.' And when she laughed: 'That's better. I'll be outside in half an hour.'

'How did you know I'd just come off duty?' she wanted to know.

'I have my spies. *Tot ziens*.'

The evening was one of unexpected pleasure. They went to a small, pleasant restaurant where the service was impeccable, the food out of this world, and where they were able to talk uninterrupted by the too close voices of those at the neighbouring tables. Alethea, who had halfheartedly chosen to wear one of her prettiest outfits was glad that she had, for the place, although small, was undoubtedly expensive and in the front rank of restaurants. They had talked easily enough, and she had found him to be one of those people with whom one could feel at home and although he touched only lightly on his home and life there she felt that she was beginning to know him quite well. And she had talked about herself too, not about Nick, that was still too painful a subject, but about her childhood and the happy years she had spent with her grandmother. Sarre had asked her if there was anyone in particular she wished to invite to their wedding. 'A register office, I'm afraid,' he had told her, 'but I'll talk to your vicar about a service afterwards—could we see him together?'

She had agreed and they settled on an evening during the week, because Alethea wouldn't have days off again until the weekend and Sarre was to return to Holland then. He had thought of everything, she reflected as she got ready for bed, all she would have to do was leave the hospital and be ready to return to Holland with him after his next visit. She would need a passport, of course, and some new clothes…she was dozing off when she came awake again with the thought that she would have to say goodbye to Nick—or perhaps it would be better if she didn't? If she hadn't been so sleepy the vexed question might have kept her awake for hours, and the next day there wasn't the time to give it a thought.

That she was leaving was already known throughout the hospital. She had been there for eight years and everyone knew her, and when she calmly told her reason for doing so she was faced with a barrage of questions. No one had quite dared to mention Nick to her face, but she was very aware that everyone longed to do so, just as they longed to ask about Mr van Diederijk's intention to marry her. After all, they had only known each other a few weeks and no one had noticed anything even faintly verging on the romantic when they had been together. And that hadn't been often. Her closer friends pointed out that neither party was of a sort to wear their heart upon their sleeve and certainly they would never air their feelings in public. And Staff, her loyal assistant and friend, declared loudly that it didn't matter what people said, love at first sight was something which happened quite often and she for her part hoped that Sister Thomas and Mr van Diederijk would live happily ever after. This view was thoroughly approved of by the majority of young ladies who worked at the hospital; they were all romantic at heart and after all, as they pointed out to each other, Sister Thomas's sudden decision to get married to someone she had only just met was just about as romantic as anyone could wish for. Alethea, who had been secretly dreading the publicity, found that she was the centre of approving interest.

It was when they were on their way down to see the vicar that Sarre slowed the car, put a hand in a pocket and handed her a little box. 'I quite forgot to give you this,' he remarked in a casual voice.

Alethea opened it. There was a ring inside, a magnificent Russian sapphire surrounded with diamonds. 'It's been in the family for a long time,' went on Sarre. 'I hope it fits.'

He put his foot down and the car shot ahead once more as she took it out and tried it on. It fitted very well and it looked quite beautiful. She thanked him quietly, smothering a pang of unhappiness that he could be so casual about something so important. But of course, it wouldn't be very important to him; he was only pandering to the conventions. She gazed at the lovely thing and couldn't help wondering what kind of a ring Nick might have given her—and surely not so casually... She said in her serene way: 'It fits very well indeed. Isn't that lucky?' She glanced at him, but he was looking ahead. 'Thank you very much, Sarre.'

He made a small sound which could have been anything and said presently: 'Does a month from today suit you? I'll be gone a week from Saturday, but there's a case I have to see the following weekend—would you like to go back with me to Groningen for a quick visit? It can only be a few days, I'm afraid, because I'm due in Hamburg very shortly. I'll bring you back, of course, and with any luck I should be able to get back here on the day before we marry.'

It was all so matter-of-fact and businesslike, although she supposed that she wouldn't have liked it any other way. She agreed to his suggestions and asked him if any of his family wanted to attend the ceremony.

'My brother. I've already told Wienand, of course. No one else. The children...' he paused, 'I think it would be best if they weren't there. You'll meet them of course when you come to stay.'

She agreed doubtfully and he began to talk about something else and made no mention of the matter again that evening.

They went first to her grandmother's house and then without waste of time to the vicarage. The vicar was an old friend of Alethea, an elderly man with a kind face and a sense of humour which was unexpected. His wife plied them with coffee while he asked questions, discussed the time of the service, suggested that a little organ music might be rather nice to have and then wrote it all down in the large diary on his desk—he was, he assured them, a very forgetful man. They left presently, everything nicely arranged, called briefly at her grandmother's once more and then drove back to London. It had all been rather a rush, but Mrs Bustle had been waiting with their supper and there had been time enough to admire the ring…

Sarre saw her to the Nurses' Home door, and wished her goodnight with the remark that he didn't expect to see much of her before he went back to Groningen. 'On the ward, of course,' he observed, 'but not to talk. If you're free on Friday evening we might get a quick meal together.'

'I'm not free,' said Alethea.

'In that case I'll wait for you in the entrance just after nine o'clock—we can get a cup of coffee somewhere.' He bent and kissed her, the light, almost businesslike kiss she was beginning to expect from him. 'Sleep well.'

He had been right; save for brief encounters on the ward, they saw nothing of each other for the next couple of days. Alethea took consolation from the admiration lavished on her ring and occupied her mind with her wedding outfit. She had had a bad moment or two when Nick had met her in one of the corridors. There had been no one about and he had stopped in front of her so that she was forced to stop too. 'Well, well,' he began, 'who'd have thought it? You're a fast worker and no mistake, Alethea, I must congratulate you.'

She chose to misunderstand him. 'Thank you, Nick,' she said gravely. 'I'm very happy…'

He had laughed at that. 'Are you, Alethea? Are you? Don't you ever think about us? You wouldn't have had a ring to dangle in front of your friends' envious eyes, but you would have had me, my dear.'

He had turned on his heel before she could answer him, and since she hadn't the faintest idea what to reply, that had been a good thing.

She would have given anything to have had a chance to talk to Sarre, but although he came to examine a patient that afternoon there was no chance to do so. She would have to wait until the next evening, although she thought that perhaps by then the smart of Nick's words would have lessened and she wouldn't want to talk about it to Sarre or anyone else.

She was late going off duty when at last the next day's work was done, and too tired to think much about her own affairs. She hurried to her room, showered and changed into the first dress that came to hand and went down to the entrance. Sarre was there, standing by the door, showing no impatience, only a quick concern because she was so late.

'I didn't have time to send you a message,' she explained. 'This case came in at the very last minute and there was a good deal to do—you know how it is…'

He smiled. 'Indeed I do. You're tired, we won't go far—there's a small restaurant close by, we could walk there. I don't know what the food's like, but we could have coffee and sandwiches.'

The restaurant proved to be an agreeable surprise. The menu was a small one, but the pork chops when they came were well cooked and the vegetables weren't straight from a deep freeze. They drank a carafe of wine with their dinner, all there was to drink except beer, and Alethea declared it to be very nice although Sarre, tasting it, declared that the beer would have been more palatable. They had apple pie and cream for afters and great cups of coffee to round off their meal. The coffee tasted of nothing much, but as Sarre observed, coffee in England so seldom did. 'Wait until you are in Groningen and you will see what I mean,' he told her, 'although I must warn you that the tea in Holland is quite different from the brew here. You'll get used to it, of course.' He leaned back in his chair, staring at her. 'Yesterday when I was on the ward you looked wretched. Why?'

She shook her head. 'Nothing—it wasn't anything.'

'Young Penrose been annoying you?'

She looked at him, trying to think of what to say, and after a moment he smiled a little. 'It was young Penrose, of course. I'm sorry,' and then: 'Does he want to make it up?'

She shook her head again. 'No.' She wanted to tell Sarre about it, but the words wouldn't come. Presently she said defiantly: 'And if he did, I wouldn't.'

He didn't smile, but she saw that he didn't quite believe her. 'I wouldn't,' she repeated vehemently.

He nodded. 'It's a pity that we weren't able to talk about it. Promise me, Alethea, that you will tell me if things worry you. Perhaps I can't help, but I can listen, and telling is half the answer, you know.'

'You're a dear,' she said warmly, 'and I was silly about it. I'm sorry.'

'Not silly. Loving someone can be the very devil. You're managing very well. There's only one more week to go, isn't there? I shall be back on Saturday of next week and we'll go over to Holland on Sunday. No,

better still, we'll go over on Saturday from Harwich—
I want to take the car, we'll have to fly another time.
Could you be ready?'

Alethea said that yes, she could, quite easily. She
would be off duty for the last time at six o'clock and
they wouldn't need to leave until eight o'clock. 'If this
weather holds it will be pleasant driving up to
Groningen in the early morning, you'll be able to see
something of the country as we go.'

She exerted herself to ask questions after that and by
the time they had strolled back to the hospital she felt
much happier. She told Sarre so and he chuckled. 'Well,
don't imagine it was my company, much more likely
to be that wine we drank.'

She laughed with him and lifted her pretty face for
his kiss. It was neither quick nor light this time. 'I hope
you will miss me,' said Sarre. 'I'm going to miss you.'

She told herself as she got ready for bed that he had
kissed her like that because she had been upset about
Nick. He really was very clever, for he must have
known that she had needed something like that to
restore her self-respect and make her feel that even if
Nick didn't want her, there were others who did. Their
marriage might work very well, she mused; in any case
it stood just as much chance as some of the marriages
among her friends, which hadn't worked well at all,
despite their declarations that they would love each
other for ever and ever.

Alethea turned restlessly in her bed. She supposed
that some couples, but not very many, really did love
each other for the rest of their lives. An enviable state,

but not for her. All the same, if Sarre and she could remain as they were, good friends and liking each other's company, then the future wasn't going to be too bad; there would be no deep feelings to hurt, no jealousy, probably no quarrelling. She thought that Sarre would be a difficult man with whom to quarrel and as she was even-tempered there should be no reason for them to fall out. She fell asleep, lapped in a feeling of security.

With Sarre gone, the week turned out to be surprisingly long; she had got used to seeing his vast form amble on to the ward and even if there had been no opportunity to talk, it had been pleasant to see him there. But as it turned out, the week, long though it seemed, wasn't long enough. The last two days of it she spent every spare moment packing up her possessions, some to be left to be fetched when she got back from Holland, some to be taken with her. She had managed to do some shopping, splashing out rather on a wedding outfit of champagne wild silk and a straw hat to go with it, a small brimmed affair with silk flowers around the crown. She would probably never wear it again, but it had looked so right… She had bought a cotton jersey two-piece to wear in Holland too; she already had an almost new lightweight coat which would go very well with it. Sarre hadn't said just how long she would be there and the weather was getting warmer every day, so she packed slacks and tops to suit all weathers, a couple of thin dresses, a skirt or two and some pretty blouses and her velvet blazer. She possessed only two evening dresses, and she packed them both, wishing as she did so that she need never again wear the one she had bought specially for Nick.

She was ready and waiting on the Saturday evening when the Porter's Lodge telephoned the Home to say that she was wanted in the front hall. She had wished her friends goodbye, thanked them for the early morning tea service which they had given her, bade goodbye to Sir Walter and her ward staff and somehow avoided meeting Nick. She went out of the Nurses' Home and into the hospital, praying fervently that she wouldn't meet him now. She almost did; she saw him coming towards her down the opposite passage to hers, both of which led to the main hall entrance. They would meet there unless she either hurried her pace or slowed down to a crawl and there was nowhere to go, she was bound to meet him. They reached the hall at the same time and she brushed past him to where she could see Sarre waiting. He had seen her too; he was beside her in a few quick strides, his hands on her shoulders, smiling down at her, while she was aware that Nick had crossed to the porter's lodge and was watching them.

'You grow prettier each time I see you,' declared Sarre, and kissed her. A quick light kiss but still a kiss. She smiled at him, knowing that Nick was still watching. 'It's been a long week,' she told him. 'I'm quite ready if you want to go now.'

He said lightly: 'Why not? I've seen everyone I needed to see. The ferry goes at ten-thirty, we'll stop and have dinner on the way. If we hurried we could go and see your grandmother if you particularly wanted to…'

She shook her head. 'I telephoned her today, she doesn't expect us, and if we went now she and Mrs Bustle would want to give us a meal and there wouldn't be time for that. I told her I'd telephone when we get back.'

'My dear girl, you can telephone her the moment we arrive home. We can talk over dinner—we have quite a few things to discuss.'

She could see out of the corner of her eye that Nick was walking away. When he had disappeared she said: 'I'll get my bag, it's in the Home still.'

'And I'll walk with you.'

And a good thing too as it turned out, for Nick must have hurried round the back of the hospital and in at the other side so that he couldn't help but meet her if she went back to the Home. He came face to face with them outside the Home door and Sarre said pleasantly: 'Ah, good evening, Penrose,' and stopped long enough to add: 'I hear that the shoulder we did is making good progress. I'll be back in a couple of weeks, but he'll be gone by then, I suppose.' He nodded a casual goodbye and opened the door for Alethea.

'I'll be here,' he told her, 'waiting.'

The Jaguar ate up the miles, heading for Harwich and the night ferry, and Alethea, sitting beside Sarre, listening to his casual conversation, felt a surge of excitement. Until that moment, everything had seemed like a dream, an improbable one which wasn't likely to come true, but it was coming true. Perhaps she should have insisted upon more time in which to make up her mind, she was suddenly beset by any number of vague fears, not one of them concrete enough to furnish her with enough material to worry over, yet all of them looming at the back of her head like a creeping fog. 'Sarre,' she began, to be instantly hushed by his:

'Don't say it, Alethea, you're scared, aren't you? It's actually happening, isn't it? and you feel as though you're being hustled and bustled into something you're suddenly not sure about. But you're not; you're coming to spend a few days with me and my family and if at the end of that time you feel you can't go through with it, then all you have to do is say so. I told you that, my dear; the door is still wide open for you to escape.'

He made it sound so logical and normal, she said at once: 'Of course you're right, Sarre—it's last-minute nerves…'

He chuckled. 'Cured by a drink and dinner! We'll stop at Marks Tey.'

They had plenty of time; they dined at leisure and then went on again, arriving exactly at the right time to go on board without a long wait. Rather to Alethea's disappointment, Sarre showed no inclination to keep her up talking; he suggested that she went straight to her cabin, told her that he had arranged for her to be called in the morning and wished her a friendly goodnight, and despite her vague peevishness at this she slept well and her good humour was quite restored by his cheerful greeting when she went on deck after her morning tea. The ferry was on the point of docking and she looked about her with interest; true, the Hoek of Holland looked very much like Harwich, but it was a foreign country and she had never travelled outside Great Britain before.

Sarre stood beside her, watching the bustle on the quay until it was time for them to get into the car, drive through Customs and finally start on their journey to Groningen.

It was still very early, not yet seven o'clock, but there was a good deal of traffic on the road. Sarre drove towards den Haag, bypassed that city and took the motorway north. He travelled at speed now until they were north of Leiden, when he turned on to the Haarlem road with the remark that they would stop for breakfast very shortly. Alethea would have been content to go on; she was hungry, but there was so much to see that that didn't seem important at the moment. All the same, when they stopped presently at a charming restaurant in the woods outside that city she discovered that she was ravenous and fell to on the rolls and toast, the thin slices of ham, the eggs and cheese with which their table was laden. 'I shall get fat,' she observed comfortably as she poured more coffee for them both. 'You don't eat a breakfast like this every morning, do you?'

Sarre nodded. 'Oh, yes—not quite as much, perhaps. You will quickly become accustomed to it.'

'Will your children be at home when we get there?'

He glanced at his watch. 'They come out of school at twelve o'clock, and we should be home well before then. If you're quite finished we might as well go.'

They didn't talk a great deal; Sarre pointed out anything which he considered might interest her and she asked questions—not as many as she would have wished, but she knew that he wanted to reach Groningen as quickly as possible and he was nice enough to slow down each time she exclaimed over something which caught her eye. It was eleven o'clock as they reached the outskirts of the city; Alethea heard the church clocks chiming the hour, one after the other. It was a pleasant welcoming sound and it made her feel a little less strange. She got out her compact and powdered her pretty face and added a little more lipstick, and was surprised to see how composed was her reflection while her insides churned with excitement and a vague fear that something would go wrong. Nothing was ever what one expected; certainly Groningen, from what she could see of it as Sarre wound his way to the centre of it, was far more beautiful than she had imagined, with its old houses bordering the canals and its lovely churches. They swept past the university and Sarre said: 'We're almost home,' and she braced herself, wondering what home would be like. She had imagined red brick, but Sarre had been telling her that many people lived in flats; perhaps he had a flat too.

He turned the car into a narrow street which converged into a wider one, lined with trees and with a narrow canal running through it; there were bridges along its length and tall important houses on both sides of the cobbles. It was quiet there and after the busyness of the main streets it was like passing into another world and age.

Sarre slowed the car and then stopped. 'Here we are,' he told her, and leaned across to open her door before getting out himself.

It wasn't red brick and it wasn't a flat, but a thin old house, towering to four storeys, its elaborate gable

crowning its flat face. The door was old too and stout,
with large windows on either side, and rows of windows
above, decreasing in size at each floor until the top one
of all, set directly under the steep gable. Alethea turned
to look at Sarre who had come round the car's bonnet
to shut her door. 'It's not a bit what I expected, it's
quite—quite beautiful and very large.'

He looked up at his home. 'It is a lovely old place,'
he conceded, 'it's also full of passages and unexpected
stairs and funny little rooms, highly inconvenient, but
I wouldn't change it for the world.' He smiled at her. 'I
hope you'll like it too, Alethea.'

'Oh, I shall!' She stared up at him earnestly. 'It's just
that I'm surprised.'

He laughed a little and took her arm as they crossed
the brick pavement and went up the three steps to the
front door. It opened as they reached it and a middle-
aged man with a merry face stood back as they went
inside.

'Welcom 'ome, guvnor, an' you, miss.' He sketched
a little bow at her and while she was still swallowing
surprise Sarre said easily: 'Ah, Al, it's good to be back.
How's everything?'

'OK, Guv.' He grinned engagingly at Sarre, who
went on: 'This is Miss Thomas, Al, my fiancée. You'll
look after her.'

'Course I will.' He gave her a friendly respectful
look. 'Right proud we are to 'ave 'er, too.' He opened
an inner door and Sarre took Alethea's arm and drew
her into the hall, a narrow lofty corridor stretching
seemingly endlessly before them. She looked round her

curiously, a little taken aback with the splendid marble-topped side tables and the panelled walls hung with paintings. There was no sign of a staircase, but when they were halfway down the hall she saw it, at right angles to the hall, a handsomely carved one, its oak treads worn by countless feet. Al had slipped ahead of them and opened another door and they went into a fair-sized room. There were no windows but light came from the enormous windows of a much larger room into which it led. Al shut the door quietly behind him and Sarre took his hand from her arm and she stood just where she was, looking about her. Nothing was as she had expected it to be. The sensation that she was having a dream, a nice one, but a dream all the same, came over her.

She looked at Sarre, standing a few paces from her, his hands in his pockets, his head a little on one side, watching her. 'Al—' she began, 'he's a Cockney! However did he get here?'

'It's a long story. He's been with me for a long time now. He's a splendid fellow, I'd trust him with my life.'

'And you've got a Scottish housekeeper.' She sounded almost accusing.

He laughed at that. 'So I have. Poor Alethea, I do believe you expected wooden shoes and baggy trousers.' He was suddenly beside her, his hands on her shoulders. 'My dear, I'm unkind to tease, but I never thought to tell you about Al—to tell you about anything, I suppose. You are always so sensible and serene...'

'Not always,' she reminded him.

CHAPTER FIVE

IT WAS IMPOSSIBLE to feel chilled for long, though. Before she had time to answer Sarre, Al was back with a tray of coffee and following hard on his heels, the housekeeper.

'Mrs McCrea,' Sarre introduced her to Alethea, 'who has been with us since I was a very small boy and is our staunch friend as well as the best house-keeper in the world.'

'Go on with you, sir,' declared Mrs McCrea comfortably, 'though I'm sure we all do our best to make you comfortable. We all wish you and Miss Thomas a long and happy life together.' She beamed at Alethea, her small bright blue eyes twinkling, and took the hand she was holding out. 'And here's a bonny girl,' she observed, 'if you'll pardon me saying so.'

Alethea smiled widely at her. They were going to like each other; Mrs McCrea was small and round and motherly and her voice was soft with the unmistakable Scottish lilt. There wasn't an ounce of guile in her and Alethea thought that probably she had never been unkind to anyone in her life. The slight chill she had felt melted and disappeared altogether at Al's warm: 'A real beaut, begging yer pardon, miss. We're proud ter 'ave yer in the 'ouse.'

A remark which she rightly took to be a compliment indeed.

'They'll be your devoted slaves,' observed Sarre when they were alone again. 'They have been urging me to marry for several years now.'

'Oh—is that why you asked me?' Alethea hated herself for asking but her tongue had run away with her.

He gave her a long look and she saw suddenly that his usually placid features could become ruthless and remote. 'No. I asked you to marry me for the reasons which I gave you. I have great regard for Al and Mrs McCrea, but neither they nor anyone else dictates my life for me.' He moved away from the chair he had been leaning against. 'Won't you sit down and have some coffee?'

Alethea stayed just where she was. 'I've annoyed you,' she said in a voice she might have used to calm a troublesome patient, 'but I'm bound to do that, aren't I? I don't know you at all well, you see. I've only just realised that you have a quite nasty temper and like your own way. I shall do my best to keep on the right side of you, but occasionally I'm bound to speak my mind.' She added reasonably: 'I'm not a doormat.'

Sarre gave a shout of laughter. 'My dear girl, thank God you're not! And you're quite right; I've a bad temper, although I endeavour to keep it within reasonable bounds, and I like my own way, too. Now sit down, do, and pour my coffee and yours.' He drew up a small velvet-covered armchair for her and pulled up a massive one for himself. 'And I know very well that you aren't a doormat. I wouldn't be marrying you if you were.'

Alethea lifted the silver coffee pot and poured the coffee into delicate cups. As she handed him a cup she observed: 'I didn't know it would be...it's rather grand.'

He glanced round him. 'Is it? I've lived here all my life and it's just home to me—I hope it will be to you.'

She answered him seriously. 'It's very beautiful. I think when I've got over my—my awe, I shall like it very much. Will you tell me about Al? How did he get here?'

Sarre crossed his long legs and stretched out comfortably. 'He was here ten years ago, chauffeuring his employer; there was an accident and he was badly injured and came into the hospital. His employer wasn't hurt and returned home, leaving Al behind. He said at the time that he would keep in touch and when Al was fit, see that he got safely back to England. He even promised him his job back, but although we tried to contact him, we never found him, so when Al was more or less fit, I took him on. He has to have osteopathy regularly and he can't drive a car for any length of time, otherwise he's pretty fit. He's most useful around the house.'

Alethea poured more coffee. 'And Mrs McCrea?'

'My mother went to school with a Scottish girl and when they married they visited each other regularly. My mother took an instant liking to Mrs McCrea on one visit and a year or two later, when her husband died suddenly, she came over here to see if she would like to live with us; she's been here ever since.'

'And is your nanny Dutch?'

'Yes—a local woman and devoted to the children. She speaks our language to them as well as Dutch.'

'Your language?'

'We have our own language in Groningen, just as they do in Friesland. It's quite different, but I expect you'll pick up a few words quickly enough.' He got up. 'You'd like to go to your room?' He tugged the bell rope by the elaborate old-fashioned stove. 'I must put in half an hour's work going through my post and telephoning the hospital. You'll be all right?'

The chill returned and she reminded herself, quite un-warrantably, that of course Sarre had work to do, she could hardly expect him to neglect it in order to entertain her. She followed Mrs McCrea up the staircase, along a gallery and into a room leading from it. It was a large apartment, with a wide, tall window draped with brocade curtains in pale pinks and blues and the same colours were repeated in the spread which covered the fourpos-ter bed, a magnificent piece of furniture, its mahogany blending with the sofa table and the huge pillow cupboard along one wall. Alone, Alethea explored, opening cupboard doors, peering into the elegant bathroom, looking out of the window and finally sitting down on the vast bed. But not for long; presently she tidied herself, brushed her hair into a curling cloud around her face, and went downstairs again. There was no sign of anyone. Perhaps she should have stayed in her room until someone came for her, but it would be silly to go back there now. She was debating which door to try when the front door opened and a young man came in.

For a split second she thought it was Sarre and then she saw that he was very much younger, not quite as tall and of a much slimmer build, and as if he read her thoughts, he crossed the hall to where she stood, crying: 'No, I'm not Sarre—I'm Wienand, his brother. And you're Alethea, even prettier than he described you.' He grinned at her and gave her a quick kiss. 'Now why didn't I see you first?'

Alethea laughed; he was so friendly and lighthearted it was impossible not to like him on sight. She offered a hand and he was still holding it when a door opened and Sarre came into the hall.

'Wienand, this is delightful, I didn't expect you as soon as this.' He smiled at them both. 'You've introduced yourselves, I see.' He turned to Alethea. 'I'm afraid I have to go out for a short while, my dear, but now that Wienand's here, you'll be perfectly all right.' He turned to his brother. 'Show her round the house, will you? and stay for lunch unless you've anything better to do…'

'I can't imagine anything better to do,' protested Wienand, and flung an arm round her shoulders. Sarre was already crossing the hall on his way to the door. His 'Tot ziens' sounded a little absent-minded and he looked faintly relieved as though he was glad that he had solved the problem of what to do with her for the time being, thought Alethea, suddenly very annoyed.

But the annoyance didn't last. She reminded herself sensibly that it wasn't as if he was in love with her. Now if it had been Nick…she brushed the dream aside and prepared to be entertained by Wienand, who proved to be an amusing companion who refused to be serious for more than a few minutes at a time. True, he answered her questions about his work; that he was indeed an osteopath and further, that he and Sarre worked closely together in a technique which the pair of them had devised, but further than that he would not go, preferring to pay her ridiculous compliments, so that she found herself laughing as she hadn't laughed for a long time. They were in the garden room now, its doors opening out on to the glorious morning, talking about nothing much in a lighthearted fashion, when Sarre came back. He greeted them affably, expressed the hope that they had amused each other, begged Alethea's pardon for leaving her and asked his brother to accompany him to his study for a few minutes.

Left to herself Alethea looked at the clock. It was ten to twelve and at midday the children came from school. The thought of meeting them for the first time on her own sent her hot and cold. She sat watching the clock, a handsome *stoelklok* with a seascape painted on its very old face, willing Sarre to come back. It was ten past the hour when she heard voices in the hall—children's voices—and braced herself for the meeting, scared stiff and at the same time resentful of Sarre's neglect. The door opened and she let out a held breath. The two men came in together and Sarre had a hand on his son's shoulder, while his little daughter, on his other side, hung on to his arm. They came straight towards her and Alethea got to her feet, feeling quite dizzy with relief.

'Alethea, here are Sarel and Jacomina.' He looked

down at the two children. 'My dears, this is Alethea Thomas, who is going to marry me within a few weeks.'

They offered hands and said 'How do you do' and smiled at her, two pairs of blue eyes staring up at her, full of hate. She hadn't expected that, but she knew enough about children to know that they were reacting in a perfectly normal way; she would have to be patient, very patient, and give them lots of time. She said now, in her pleasant, soft voice: 'How do you do, Sarel—Jacomina, I'm very glad to meet you. I hope that when we have got to know each other, we shall be good friends.'

They didn't answer, and Sarre, who had turned away to say something to his brother but had obviously been listening, observed: 'Oh, I'm sure of that. Now you had both better go up to Nanny and tidy yourselves for lunch.'

'Yes, Papa, and may we take Alethea with us to meet Nanny?'

Sarre hesitated. 'There's not much time—Alethea wants a drink with us, Nanny might keep her.'

'We won't let her, Papa. Just two minutes, please...'

He smiled down at them. 'Well, what does Alethea say?'

'I'd like to meet Nanny,' said Alethea promptly, and wondered what was in store for her. She was soon to know. They were on their way upstairs when Sarel asked: 'Do you speak our language, Alethea?'

She glanced at him. He was a good-looking little boy with his father's fine features and blue eyes. His hair was the colour of lint and he had the endearing boniness of all small boys. He returned her look with a limpid one of his own and then smiled when she said: 'Not one word. I hope you'll both help me to learn it, Sarel.'

'You and Nanny won't be able to understand each other,' observed Jacomina with satisfaction. She was like her father too, a fact which for some reason was a relief to Alethea; she supposed she didn't want to be reminded of his first wife.

'Then we'll just have to smile at each other, won't we?' said Alethea sensibly.

They had walked the length of the gallery and started up a second smaller staircase to the floor above. There was another gallery here with rooms leading from it and Sarel opened one of the doors and invited her inside. As she went past him Alethea paused. 'Tell me, Sarel,' she asked, 'where did you both learn to speak such good English?'

'Papa and Mrs McCrea and Al—they all speak English to us. Here's Nanny.'

The room was obviously the children's. It was large, furnished comfortably with small chairs, a large round table, and had cupboards built into its walls. There was a rocking horse by the window and a superb dolls' house and the walls were hung with maps, a variety of Beatrix Potter prints and over the closed stove, a very large cuckoo clock. It was a cosy room and Alethea smiled as she gazed round her. But the middle-aged woman standing by the stove wasn't smiling, she was staring hard, her rather grim face set sternly. She was tall and angular, her hair so fair that the grey with which it was sprinkled could hardly be seen. She was dressed soberly in a plain brown dress, and she smoothed the skirt now, waiting for Alethea to say something. The children stood silently and she realised that they had no intention of speaking. She went across the room and held out a hand.

'I'm Alethea Thomas,' she said. 'How do you do, Nanny?'

Her hand was taken but the stern features didn't relax. Nanny said something Alethea couldn't understand and spoke to the children, who chorused in answer and disappeared through a door at the other end of the room.

Alethea, left alone with Nanny, smiled at her again and then wandered off round the room, examining its contents. It appeared to house every kind of toy and game that a child could wish for; she had never seen such a splendid collection in all her life. She was peering at the dolls' house when the children returned, and ignoring their quick, enquiring look, she said calmly: 'Oh, hullo, there you are. What wonderful toys you have. If you're ready should we be getting back to your papa?'

The children said something to Nanny and she answered briefly and then nodded just as briefly at Alethea, who nonetheless wished her goodbye for all the world as though they were the best of friends, and then accompanied the children downstairs again, talking cheerfully the whole way, trying not to mind their monosyllabic replies.

The men got up as they entered the garden room and Sarre brought her a sherry. 'Did the children introduce you to Nanny?' he wanted to know, 'and I hope they translated for you both—their English is pretty good.'

'It's super,' declared Alethea. 'Nanny must be a marvellous person. I expect she loves them very much.'

He had pulled up a chair beside her. 'Oh, she does—she spoils them too,' he smiled at her. 'That's where you come in, my dear.'

The children were sitting with their uncle, but near enough to hear their father's conversation. Alethea said carefully: 'No one could ever take Nanny's place. She's something special, isn't she?'

She was aware as she spoke that the children had heard her, were listening to every word she uttered, would in fact do so while she was in their father's house. Perhaps, she mused hopefully, by the time she was married to Sarre, they would be used to the idea.

They went in to lunch presently, a meal served in a lofty panelled room with a large circular table to seat sixteen people and a great carved sideboard taking up the whole of one wall. The one tall window was draped with rich crimson velvet curtains and matched the glowing colours of the carpet, reflected in a more subdued manner by the portraits on the walls. The whole made a fitting background for the white table linen and shining silver and glass.

Al waited at table, assisted by a cheerful young girl. He was excellent at his job too, Alethea discovered. For all his funny Cockney manner, he was now the picture of a dignified manservant. And the food was delicious. Alethea, hungry after their journey and all the excitement, ate with pleasure, exchanging light-hearted conversation with Wienand and rather more serious remarks with Sarre. He seemed older now that he was in his own home and a little remote, but his smile when he looked at her was just as friendly. Towards the end of the meal he told her: 'I simply must go to my rooms this afternoon—will you forgive me if I leave you alone? We'll go out this evening if you wish, or stay home, just as you like…'

'I'd like to stay here,' said Alethea promptly, 'and be taken round the house. We didn't have time…'

'Of course…the children go to bed at half past seven and I usually dine at eight o'clock if I'm in. Will that suit you?'

'Oh, yes. You don't have to go to the hospital this evening?'

He shook his head. 'No—not unless something turns up. What will you do with yourself this afternoon? The children will be at school, I'm afraid, but Al could drive you round if you would like that.'

'I'd rather walk,' she said promptly, 'if I could have the address of this house written down just in case I get lost…'

And so she walked, seen out of the house in a fatherly way by Al, who having issued a series of warnings about traffic on the wrong side of the road and not falling into canals, stood at the door until she was at the end of the quiet street. She turned and waved to him just before she went round the corner.

The city was easy enough to find one's way about. Al had assured her there were two large squares into which the main streets converged, so that it would be impossible to get lost. Alethea, wandering happily from one to the other, got lost a dozen times, but there was always the tall spire of St Martin's church acting as a towering landmark to guide her. The shops were enticing and worthy of a much longer visit, she discovered as she began to wend her way back to Sarre's house, but she would have ample time to shop. Sarre would be at the hospital or his rooms each day, she imagined, and the children at school; she would be left largely to her own devices.

She was wrong. Sarre returned home very shortly after she herself did, to find her sitting alone in the small sitting room Al had invited her to use. The children, Al informed her, were in their own playroom where they had their tea with Nanny and he promised her a nice English tea in a brace of shakes. Before he could bring it, however, Sarre joined her.

'You must think that you've been entirely forgotten,' he observed, 'and I'm sorry, although I suppose being a nurse you understand that my time isn't my own. But I've arranged to be free tomorrow afternoon so that I can show you the countryside, and in the morning perhaps you would like to come to the clinic with me. Wienand is in charge of it and I send those patients who I think might benefit to him there. I've beds in the orthopaedic hospital, of course, and quite a large private practice.'

He stretched out in a large wing chair opposite her, looking relaxed and not in the least tired, and when Al brought the tea presently and she had poured it and handed him a cup, he said comfortably: 'This is nice, I had quite forgotten how pleasant it is to come home to someone waiting for me. Are the children in?'

She felt as though she had been his wife for years. 'Yes, upstairs having their tea with Nanny; Al says they always do.'

Sarre bit into one of Mrs McCrea's scones. 'They usually come down when I'm home, but I expect they're a little shy.' He smiled at her. 'They'll not be that for long. How did you find them?'

He wasn't looking at her. A large shaggy dog was peering at them through the window and Sarre got up to let him in. 'Rough—hullo, old fellow! Alethea, he was in the kitchen when we arrived and I took him with me in the car—you've not met him.'

Alethea liked dogs; she scratched his ear for him and he looked up at her with instant friendliness. 'He's a poppet,' she declared, glad that his entry had saved her having to answer Sarre about the children. Of course they weren't shy, she thought silently; they were being unfriendly, but whether they were prepared to let their father see that, she had yet to discover.

It seemed that they weren't, for when they joined them presently in the sitting room they were the very soul of politeness, asking her questions about England, telling her about school, wanting to know about the wedding…and all the time looking at her with an enmity which left her both puzzled and a little frightened. Frightened that they would never like her, never accept her into the family. But she had plenty of spirit; she told herself that probably she was imagining the whole thing just because she had been so anxious that they should like her. They might be jealous, afraid that she was going to take the lion's share of their father from them. She was quite relieved to have hit on a likely reason, and when Sarre suggested that she might like to go to his study and telephone her grandmother, she agreed with alacrity. He might be just as anxious to have his children to himself as they were to be with him.

Sarre left her once he had got the number and she settled down to a brief chat with her grandparent. Everything was lovely, she declared, the house was a dream, the children were very like Sarre in looks and with such beautiful manners… She talked away for five minutes until she felt that she had satisfied her grandmother's interest, asked a few questions about home, promised to telephone again, and rang off.

She didn't go back to the sitting room at once; ten minutes wasn't long enough. She got up from Sarre's great leather chair and wandered round the room, having a good look. It was as lofty as the other rooms in the house, a long, rather narrow room reached by a short passage from the hall, its windows overlooking the side of the house. She paused to look out on to the high wall which ran its length, a neat flower bed, gay with colour, between it and the flag path which ran beneath the window. She wondered where it went and then resumed her tour. There were bookshelves, of course, stuffed with books, mostly medical, in Dutch, German and English. There were some rather lovely engravings on the walls, a desk piled high with books, papers, professional samples, photos of the children and an enormous diary, and a nice little chair drawn up to a small worktable, a charming Regency trifle with a green moiré bag hanging from its frame. Alethea stopped short: perhaps his first wife had sat there, embroidering, while he worked at the desk. She ran her hand over the back of the velvet-covered chair, not liking to sit in it. He wouldn't want her to anyway, and even if he did, she had never done embroidery in her life, she wouldn't know where to begin. She made an instant resolve to try her hand at it at the first opportunity. She was standing irresolutely in the middle of the room when Sarre came back.

'Finished?' he wanted to know. 'We were wondering what had happened to you.'

She didn't try to explain, only smiled, assured him that she had indeed finished and accompanied him back to the sitting room. The children went away shortly afterwards—to do their homework, they explained. They wished her goodnight in their almost perfect English, and then lapsed into rather noisy Dutch, begging their father to do something or other.

'There's this habit we have acquired,' he explained, laughing. 'They like me to go upstairs and wish them goodnight. I shall hand it over to you once we're married, Alethea.'

She saw the instant anger in their young faces. 'Oh, I don't know,' she observed mildly, 'I think it sounds like a very pleasant custom. I'll think up one for myself.' She smiled at him. 'My father tucked me up when I was small.'

His blue eyes twinkled. 'I can think of several answers to that, Alethea. If I were ten years younger and not so very out of practice, I might have tried one of them.'

She went faintly pink and then lost her pretty colour when she remembered that Nick might have made just such a remark. It was disconcerting when Sarre said softly: 'You're remembering again, Alethea, you are forgetting what I said about turning the page.'

'I can't think why you put up with me,' she told him shyly. 'I really must pull up my socks.'

The children had been listening, and now Sarel exclaimed: 'But you do not wear socks, Alethea,' which set them all laughing so that just for a few moments they weren't hating her at all—indeed, they went upstairs, still laughing about the little joke, leaving Sarre and her together.

'There's half an hour before we need to change,' said Sarre cheerfully. 'Shall we go into the garden? It isn't large, but it's pretty.' And once there, walking between the well-tended borders: 'I quite forgot to tell you, there are one or two friends coming this evening: my partner and his wife, Wienand, of course, and his current girlfriend, Doctor and Mevrouw Ardsch—he works with me a great deal, you'll like his wife, and Doctor Singma and Doctor van Wevelen. Anna Singma is my assistant and van Wevelen is the senior anaesthetist.'

'Oh,' said Alethea faintly, 'are they coming to dinner?'

'Yes. I thought it would be more fun for you if we had something of a party.'

She agreed at once, a little hurt that her company wasn't sufficient to amuse him on his first evening home, but he looked so pleased at his little surprise that she forced herself to a delight she didn't feel.

'I know we had decided to dine alone and go round the house, but anyone can go with you some time or other and it's a good opportunity to meet some of the people you'll be seeing a good deal of in the future. Anna thought it was a splendid idea.'

Anna did, did she? thought Alethea, her mind busy with what she should wear. The grey crêpe, she decided, and those expensive grey satin sandals which matched it so perfectly.

They parted presently and Alethea set about the business of making the most of herself, a not too difficult task, and as though everything was on her side for once, her hair went like a dream, her make-up presented no problems and the grey crêpe looked better than ever. She surveyed herself without conceit in the pier-glass in her room and went downstairs.

Sarre was in his study, the door was standing open and she could see him at the end of the passage at his desk, but he must have been listening for her because he came to join her in the hall at once. 'You look good enough to eat,' he observed.

She just managed not to say it to him, too. Her sober: 'Thank you,' masked her admiration. He looked splendid; he might not be so very young any more, but any woman would be glad to catch his eye and gain his attention. Alethea touched her engagement ring and felt a little thrill of satisfaction. At least she had his attention, or some of it at any rate.

'Let's have a drink while we're waiting,' said Sarre, and took her across the hall to a room she hadn't seen— an enormous drawing room with walls hung with straw-coloured silk, a highly ornamental plaster ceiling, two large windows elaborately draped with the same straw-coloured silk, an Aubusson carpet like a flower garden and grouped upon it, chairs and sofas covered in old rose and pale, silvery green.

'What an absolutely gorgeous room!' cried Alethea, quite taken aback.

'You like it? I'm fond of it myself; we shall use it more often once we are married, for naturally we shall entertain more.'

He had gone over to an exquisite sofa table where a tray of drinks stood. 'What will you have?'

They were sipping their drinks when Wienand arrived, accompanied by a rather languid girl with frizzed hair and wearing what looked exactly like a silver tissue tent. 'Marthe,' said Wienand by way of introduction. 'Alethea, you look divine.' He looked at his companion. 'Darling, why can't you wear a dress that shows a bit of you sometimes?'

'It's a lovely dress,' said Alethea, and was surprised to discover that Marthe was a little shy and uncertain of herself after all, for she gave her a rather timid thankful smile and said in a breathless voice: 'Oh, do you really think so? You look lovely.'

'Thank you. What very good English you speak—I feel a complete idiot not understanding Dutch.'

'You'll soon pick it up,' declared Sarre, and turned to greet his partner Doctor Jaldert and his wife Hilde, a pleasant couple who at once bombarded Alethea with friendly questions. The Ardschs came in next, Pieter and Sita, and hard on their heels Doctor van Wevelen and Anna Singma.

Alethea greeted the former first, surreptitiously taking note of their last guest—a tall, striking woman, a few years older than Alethea, she judged, and handsome too. She was dressed expensively and in excellent taste, but Alethea couldn't help her pleasure at seeing that her figure was deplorable. How mean can I get? she thought as she shook Anna's hand and smilingly thanked her for her good wishes, and then decided that she could get a whole lot meaner when Anna put a hand on Sarre's arm and kissed him.

Someone must have worked very hard to make the evening a success. The dinner was a splendid one, there was champagne, drunk from crystal glasses, and brandy which went straight to Alethea's head, with their coffee. But it wasn't only the food, everyone there obviously knew everyone else very well indeed, and Alethea was conscious that they were all making her welcome in their circle. Her doubts, vague but persistent, began to melt away, the future looked warm and welcoming.

They saw their guests off together and then Sarre closed the heavy old door and took her arm. 'Another drink before bed?' he suggested, and led the way back to the drawing room. 'And what do you think of my friends, my dear?'

'They're super.' She accepted, recklessly, a glass of champagne. 'They could have made me feel...' she sought for a word, 'well, out of it, but they treated me as though they had known me for years.'

'They liked you,' his voice was kind. 'And they all think you're very beautiful. And you are, Alethea.'

She looked at him like a child who had pleased a grown-up. 'I'm glad you think so, Sarre. I hope you will always be proud of me. I shall do my best.'

He had come much closer to her. 'I do think so, and I am proud of you.' He took her glass from her and bent to kiss her. Probably it was the champagne which made it seem different this time, she thought a trifle wildly.

'I think I'll go to bed,' she told him. 'It was a lovely evening—the whole day's been super. Goodnight, Sarre.'

He stepped back, smiling a little. 'Goodnight, my dear.'

She was at the door when she turned to ask: 'Have you known Anna a long time, Sarre?'

She almost didn't wait for his answer, for she hadn't meant to ask him that. All that champagne... She tried to look casual as though the answer didn't matter in the least, so that she didn't see the look of surprise and then amusement which swept over Sarre's calm face. 'Oh, years,' his voice was bland, 'she's a brilliant surgeon— a woman doing orthopaedics is unusual, you know— we're very old friends.' He paused, and shot Alethea a quick hard look. 'A good thing, as we see so much of each other.'

Alethea, a little top-heavy with champagne, just stopped herself in time from wanting to know why he hadn't chosen to marry Anna, since they were such old friends. Instead she said in a clear voice: 'She is a very handsome woman and it must be wonderful to be a good surgeon and striking to look at too,' she added for good measure. 'Her clothes are lovely.'

And when Sarre didn't answer, only smiled slightly, she whisked herself through the door. She left it open and she was almost at the top of the staircase when she heard Sarre close it.

Alethea slept dreamlessly until Nel brought her her

early morning tea, smiling and nodding at the early
morning sunshine which filled the room. It was already
half past seven. Alethea swallowed her tea and raced
through a shower; she was going with Sarre to the clinic
and she mustn't keep him waiting. She put on the cotton
jersey outfit, a modicum of make-up, brushed her hair
free of tangles and hurried downstairs.

In the hall she paused. There were a number of
doors, one or two of them were slightly open; she knew
the sitting room and the drawing room and the study,
the others were unknown quantities. She was about to
try the first one when Sarre's voice reached her. 'In
here, Alethea—right-hand middle door.'

It was a small room with no window, getting its light
from the drawing room beyond the open double doors.
Sarre got up as she went in and pulled out a chair as he
wished her a cheerful good morning. She sat down at
the small oval table and he asked: 'Tea or coffee?
There's coffee here, but I have it on the best authority—
Al—that Mrs McCrea is poised over a teapot with the
kettle in case you would prefer tea.'

She laughed. 'I had a super cup of tea just now. I'd
like coffee, please.'

She was taking the first sip when Al sidled through
the door. His 'Morning, miss,' was chirpy, but then she
supposed he always was. 'A nice rasher and an egg or
two?' he suggested, 'or there's a bit of 'am…'

Her eyes swept the table. There was marmalade and
toast and orange juice—she was expected to have the
bacon and eggs. She told him one egg and two rashers
and he slipped out of the room. Only when they heard

the faint creak of the baize service door did Sarre remark: 'We've gone all British, as you see, only the warm weather saves us from plates of porridge. Did you sleep?'

'Like a log. When do you want to go to the clinic?'

He glanced at his watch. 'In about half an hour. Does that suit you?'

'Of course. Don't the children come to breakfast?'

He shook his head. 'Nanny says they don't eat properly unless she's there to see that they do.' He glanced at her. 'Perhaps that's something you'll be able to alter later on. They're getting too old for her. I wouldn't dream of sending her away, but I'd like her to stop babying them both.'

He didn't say any more because Al came back then, and she was thankful that she didn't have to answer him. Life was going to be rather wonderful in this lovely old house, but it was going to hold a few pitfalls too.

But she forgot all this in the morning's interest. The clinic was on the other side of the city, on its very edge, so that the grounds merged into the green countryside. It had a large outpatients' department as well as several wards and a wing of private rooms. Alethea, very much interested, poked her pretty nose everywhere, asking endless questions of both Sarre and Wienand, and then went and sat in Sarre's office while he and his brother went away to see their patients. From what she had seen the whole scheme seemed to be working extremely well, and she was impressed. It was unusual for orthopaedic surgery and osteopathy to join forces so closely, but it appeared to work well. The clinic, she had been told, had been going for five years now and Wienand had told her proudly that their treatment had resulted in success for at least seventy per cent of their patients. 'And that doesn't include the improvements,' he added. 'Of course, not all Sarre's patients are suitable, but the younger ones especially react very well.'

'And the older ones?' she had wanted to know.

'I get them first, before operation, I knock them into shape, as it were, control their diet, give them massage, exercises, osteopathy.'

And later, when Sarre had finished his work there and they were driving back to the house, he told her more. He didn't exaggerate or enthuse as Wienand had done, but she sensed that he was completely confident in the work they were doing at the clinic.

'And do you think the idea will catch on in England?' she wanted to know.

'Yes. Sir Walter is enthusiastic—so is a surgeon in Hamburg. That's where I have to go in a few days' time—five, to be exact. I'll take you back first, of course. I'm afraid we shan't be able to go away at present, Alethea, I've a good deal of work lined up and probably I shall have to go back to Hamburg within a few weeks. Perhaps you would like to come with me?'

'Yes, please. But what about Sarel and Jacomina?'

'We'll manage some kind of a holiday with them during their summer break. I've a boat on the lakes in Friesland, we could spend a few days on her. Do you sail?'

Alethea admitted with a sinking heart that she didn't.

Her knowledge of boats was non-existent and she wasn't sure that she wanted to know anything about them, anyway.

She felt a little reassured that afternoon, though, for they went to Sneeker Mere and he showed her the boat, a sturdy *botter*, which looked reassuringly safe and extremely comfortable to boot. That evening the children had dinner with them and they talked about the holidays and Alethea, ignoring their angry blue eyes, agreed to all Sarre's plans for a few days' sailing *en famille*.

And after that the remaining days flew by. Sarre was away from home for a good deal of the day and they didn't dine alone; either the children joined them for a special treat or Wienand, or on the last night of all, Anna, making a rather uneasy party of three. She had apologised for dining with them, but as she had pointed out to Alethea, there were one or two questions which had to be settled before Sarre went to Hamburg and there hadn't been time at the hospital. So the conversation was largely in her hands and his, and although Alethea was included as often as possible, she couldn't help but feel rather out of it.

But Sarre had made up for it afterwards; they were to go on the following evening and he would have to operate as usual in the morning and see his patients in the afternoon. 'So we shan't see much of each other tomorrow,' he told her, taking her hands in his. 'I've enjoyed every moment of being with you, my dear. It only remains for you to tell me if you still want to marry me.'

'Well, I do.'

He smiled and kissed her, briefly and coolly as though it didn't matter much. 'Good. And I'm sure the children are delighted with you, just as everyone else is.'

'They're all absolutely super,' she told him warmly. Wild horses wouldn't have made her tell him about the horror of finding one of Sarel's white rats in her bed the night before. She had seen the covers moving and had almost died of fright before she dared to pull them slowly down and disclose the small animal. And even though it had been late she had nerved herself to pick it up and carry it all the way upstairs to Sarel's room. The light was still on, for the door wasn't quite shut; she had knocked gently and gone in to find the boy with his eyes closed, but not, she had been sure, asleep. She had touched him lightly on a bony shoulder and somehow or other managed to sound as though carrying rats around the house late at night was commonplace to her.

'I found him in my room,' she told him. 'He's frightened out of his life, poor little beast—I expect someone left a door open. Where would you like me to put him?'

The blue eyes regarded her with surprise and something like respect.

'I'll have him.' Sarel had got out of bed and taken the creature in his hand, and Alethea had shuddered strongly as it crept into his pyjama sleeve.

'Don't you mind rats?' asked Sarel.

'Well, they're not my favourite pet,' she had answered cheerfully, 'but he's rather nice, isn't he? What's his name?'

'Caesar.' Sarel had scowled suddenly and turned his back on her. 'Thank you for bringing him back. Goodnight.'

Alethea had said goodnight in a normal voice and gone back to her room.

CHAPTER SIX

AFTER THE SPACE and grandeur of Sarre's home, Alethea found her grandmother's cottage Lilliputian, especially while Sarre was with her, for his head missed the ceiling by inches and he filled the small rooms with his size. But it was nice to be home again, to be hugged and made much of by Mrs Thomas and Mrs Bustle. And the journey back with Sarre had been unexpectedly fun; she had thought of him as a rather quiet man and a delightful companion, but not given to the light-hearted banter indulged in by Wienand, and she was at first rather surprised and then delighted at an apparently unending stream of anecdotes about himself and his family, some of them quite outrageous, and mingled in with them charming little tales of his children.

They had crossed on the night ferry from the Hoek and arrived at the cottage in time for a late breakfast, a long-drawn-out meal because the two older ladies wanted a blow-by-blow account of Alethea's holiday and now that Sarre was to be one of the family, questions were fired at him too, all of which he answered with the greatest good nature.

It was later when Alethea had unpacked and shown Sarre his room that they fell to discussing the wedding and since he would have to return on the evening of the following day, the two of them left the older ladies over their coffee, and strolled down to the village, to make sure that the vicar had the time and the date right. It was a pleasant day and they didn't hurry, and when they had been to the vicarage they decided to continue their walk; lunch was to be later than usual, and they had plenty of time.

They went round the side of the church and up a narrow rutted lane winding away into the quiet country around the village, talking of nothing in particular, and Alethea felt how restful Sarre was to be with. He wasn't Nick, of course, but he had shown that he could be very amusing and never, she had noted, at anyone's expense, and he never criticised her appearance. If her hair was coming loose, he merely tucked the end behind an ear or brushed it back without a word and he remembered to tell her that she looked nice. With a pang she remembered the evening in the restaurant when everything had gone wrong; Nick hadn't noticed her new dress. It was strange, she mused, that Sarre, who didn't appear to notice anything, made all the right remarks about her clothes, and Nick, who was an expert on such matters, had never got beyond a vague: 'That's nice.' Following her train of thought she said aloud: 'I've bought a new outfit for the wedding. I hope you'll like it.'

He looked down at her, smiling lazily. 'I'm sure I shall—is it to be a surprise?'

'Well, yes. It's supposed to be, you know. Though it

really doesn't matter—I mean, it's not quite the same as…'

He laughed a little. 'You mean that we are both past the stage of white satin and veils and hordes of brides-maids. Should you have liked that?'

Alethea recoiled in horror. 'Lord, no! I'm twenty-seven, Sarre—besides, how can one possibly enjoy one's wedding if one is fussing about veils and bouquets and guests?'

'You intend to enjoy our wedding?'

'Yes. Don't you?' She added hastily: 'That was a silly thing for me to ask. I'm sorry…I was only thinking—we're friends and I feel comfortable with you and you know all about me. I don't know much about you and I only want to know what you wish to tell me—I'll never encroach, I promise you, Sarre.' She added thoughtfully: 'Being friends is very restful.'

He glanced down at her. 'Yes, so much more restful than being in love.'

She went pink. 'Yes. Will you fly over for the wedding?'

'No—Wienand and I will drive and he'll fly back. We'll get here the evening before. Which reminds me, I wanted to ask you about witnesses at the register office. Who would you like? Your grandmother, natu-rally—is there anyone else?'

'No. I haven't any aunts or cousins. Would any of your family like to come or would they prefer not to?'

'I'm sure they would like it. I'll ask them. Wienand will be with us, of course.' He took her arm. 'I thought we might invite Sir Walter and his wife too.'

'Are we going straight back?' she asked.

'Would you mind? I do have quite a backlog of patients. I shall be going to Hamburg, though, in a couple of weeks' time, I thought you might come too.'

'I shall like that.'

They turned their steps homewards then, talking casually, but not about themselves. There didn't seem any more to say, and indeed for the rest of that day and the few hours they had together before he left for Holland again, they scarcely mentioned their wedding. It was as if Sarre, now that all the arrangements had been made, had lost all interest in it. Alethea didn't allow herself to mind about this; after all, he was a man at the height of his career with wide interests, he had made his mark in the world, he had his home and children, all that was behind him, whereas a younger man would probably see his wedding as the beginning of these things. Nick, for example—she tried to bury the thought and couldn't—there would have been a house to search for and furnish, a career to plan, children to educate and bring up... She made herself stop thinking about it. Sarre had told her to turn the page forward, and she must.

She missed Sarre when he went; the little house had seemed over-full while he was there but curiously empty when he was no longer there. She occupied herself in sorting out her clothes and packing those she would take with her, conferring with her grandmother and Mrs Bustle about the lunch which was to be given after the ceremony, and helping to clean the little house from top to bottom, a quite unnecessary exercise which

Mrs Bustle considered absolutely essential before the wedding could take place.

In actual fact, the days flew by. Sarre had telephoned her from Hamburg and there had been an elaborate card from Mrs McCrea and another from Al and she had received a surprising number from her friends at Theobald's. She had hoped that there might have been something from the children and had to remind herself that she was still almost a stranger to them. Patience, she told herself once more; they hardly knew each other as yet.

Sarre and Wienand arrived together in the afternoon, having made the crossing from Calais by Hovercraft, and Alethea, seeing the Jaguar slide to a halt at the gate, hurried out to meet them, and if she was disappointed at Sarre's quick kiss it was instantly made up for by Wienand's boisterous hug and warm salute. 'Prettier than ever,' he declared. 'How do you fancy switching bridegrooms tomorrow?'

'What about the girlfriend?' asked Alethea, laughing.

'Which one?' he laughed. They were walking up the path, the three of them together, and Alethea's grandmother, watching them from the window, frowned a little before going to meet them.

They had tea in the garden, one of Mrs Bustle's special teas, with scones and jam and cream, ginger cake, cucumber sandwiches and little iced biscuits, and now the conversation was all of the wedding. 'There will be an aunt and uncle of mine coming,' explained Sarre, 'my father's brother and his wife. They'll drive up from London in the morning in time for the church service— you already know about Sir Walter and his wife.'

'Well, I haven't invited anyone,' said Alethea, 'if I'd asked one of my friends at Theobald's they would all have expected to come. There's just Granny and Mrs Bustle and the vicar's wife…'

'And the entire village, unless I'm very much mistaken,' remarked her grandmother dryly.

Alethea and Sarre went for a walk after tea, leaving Wienand to entertain her grandmother, and Alethea asked how the children were.

'Very well—you didn't meet Nero, their dachshund, did you? He was at the vet's—he came home yesterday and they're all over him.'

She made some noncommittal answer, wondering if he had deliberately misunderstood her, and told him about the cards. 'I've saved all of them for you to see,' she added, and then wondered if they would interest him at all. She still didn't know when he said: 'We'll put them in a scrapbook, shall we?' and went on to talk about something else.

It seemed strange to be walking down the churchyard path with Sarre the next morning, his ring on her finger. Alethea didn't feel married yet, though; the ceremony at the register office had been formal and almost businesslike—she was glad that only her grandmother and Wienand had been there as witnesses, because none of it had seemed quite real. But Sarre was real enough, walking beside her now in his beautiful pale grey suit. He was holding her hand and halfway up the path he stopped and turned her round to face him.

'You look quite lovely,' he told her, 'the most lovely

bride that ever was.' He smiled down at her. 'And now we're going to be married.'

She smiled back at him. 'Oh, Sarre, do you feel like that too? I'm so glad. I don't think I like register offices much.'

He lifted her hand and kissed it. 'I promise you we'll not go to one again, my dear.'

At the porch the vicar was waiting and over his shoulder Alethea saw that her grandmother had been quite right; the church was full. She said, 'Oh, lord!' under her breath and was glad of the reassuring grip of Sarre's hand on hers. He let go of it for a moment and turned to pick up something on the porch bench; a posy of flowers exactly matching her outfit. She took it in her other hand and caught his again as they started down the aisle.

It was a simple ceremony and brief, yet she felt well and truly married as they came out of the church with everyone crowding round them wishing them well, throwing confetti and rose petals, calling good luck. They brushed each other down, laughing, when they got back to the cottage and then went to the door to meet their few guests. Sarre's aunt and uncle were dears, elderly and good-natured and pleased with everything. They had arrived in an elderly Rolls-Royce driven by a man called Piet, no longer young but thickset and so broad that he appeared to be almost square. Sarre greeted him like an old friend, introduced Alethea who had a hand almost wrung off before Piet was led away by Mrs Bustle for a cooling draught of beer, and then took her to join the others.

The lunch was a happy affair with everyone crowded round the table in the dining room. Mrs Bustle had excelled herself with iced melon, fresh salmon salad, and a variety of rich puddings. Sarre had insisted on providing the champagne and Alethea, still feeling as though she were in a dream, drank two glasses of it before she quite knew what she was doing. Sarre, sitting beside her and glancing down, chuckled at her pink cheeks and bright eyes. 'You need a slice of wedding cake to mop up the champagne,' he said softly. 'It's coming in now and you'll have to cut it.'

She managed very well, although it seemed a great pity to spoil such a lovely bride cake. It was so good that Sarre gave her another glass of champagne and she sat listening to the speeches in a pleasant haze. Wienand proposing their health, Sarre replying, his uncle getting up and welcoming her into the family, even the vicar saying a word or two. They came to an end at last and everyone went into the garden and sat about and talked until Mrs Bustle, with a little discreet help from a girl from the village, came out with the tea tray and after that it was time to leave. They were going from Dover this time, with the Hovercraft, an early evening crossing which meant that they would be back in Groningen well before midnight.

Sitting in the car presently with Sarre beside her, Alethea sighed and said: 'Well, that was a very nice wedding. I quite enjoyed it.'

'So did I. I'm glad Uncle and Aunt are taking your grandmother and Mrs Bustle out to dinner this evening, it'll make a nice end to the day.'

Alethea agreed. And what sort of an end could she expect for her day? she wondered. The children would be in bed, probably the servants as well. Were they going to stop on the way for dinner, or have supper when they arrived? She didn't like to ask and upon reflection, it didn't really matter.

She was still wearing her wedding outfit although she had left the bouquet with her grandmother. Sarre had asked her to keep it on and although she hadn't planned to wear it on the journey she had had no objection; they would be in the car for the whole journey so that there was no fear of spoiling it.

'We have a long drive before us,' explained Sarre, 'but once we're on the other side we can speed up a bit.'

As to speed, Alethea decided in no time at all, they weren't doing too badly on this side either. Sarre cut across to the M11, left it just south of Harlow and worked his way down to the Dartford Tunnel, and after that it was a more or less straight run all the way to Dover, with the Jaguar eating up the miles with no effort at all.

'This is a nice car,' observed Alethea.

Sarre's mouth twitched. 'Very nice,' he agreed gravely. 'I need something pretty powerful; I travel around quite a bit. I've just taken delivery of a Bristol 603E, we'll try it out together.'

Alethea thought a bit. 'A Bristol—aren't they handmade, as it were?'

'That's right.' He added: 'I need two cars in case one breaks down.'

She didn't know much about cars, but surely a Bristol and a Jaguar would add up to around thirty-five thousand pounds? It occurred to her that she had very little knowledge of Sarre's income. He had told her that he had inherited the house in Groningen, and doctors, she knew, did get discount on things, but there were still the servants and the upkeep of the big house. She longed to ask about it and didn't dare.

'We've not discussed money, have we?' remarked Sarre, just as though he had known what she was thinking about, so that she went a guilty red and jumped. She said: 'No,' rather shortly and then added: 'You don't have to, unless you want to.'

He laughed softly. 'My dear girl, you are my wife, of course we must discuss it.'

He sent the car tearing down the M2. 'We'll go and see my solicitor as soon as possible—I've made a new will, of course.'

'Sarre…'

'It's customary,' he pointed out laconically. 'It will be explained to you in good time. I've money of my own as well as an income from my work—quite a lot of money. You'll have an allowance, naturally, and I think I can promise that you can have anything within reason.'

'Are you rich?' asked Alethea.

'Well, yes, I'm afraid I am. It seemed best not to mention it until after we were married.' She could hear the laugh in his voice as he spoke.

'Very rich?'

'Very.'

She sat silent for all of a minute. 'If I'd known that I'm not sure if I would have married you.'

'That's why I waited until we were married before telling you.'

He was looking straight ahead and she stared at his profile, its chin very firm, his mouth too. As she looked it curved into a smile. 'Forgiven?' he wanted to know.

He couldn't see her smile, but she did. 'Yes, of course. Actually, I expect I'll like it very much—I mean, to have money to spend.'

She settled back in her seat; she felt more at ease with him now that she knew. Money wasn't all that important to her, but it would be nice to have enough of it; besides, Sarre seemed to take it for granted and she supposed that in time she would too.

The crossing was smooth; it seemed no time at all before they were making their way out of Calais towards Ostend and then on towards Antwerp. They stopped in Bruges where they had dinner at the Portinari Hotel, not lingering over it, and then sped on. From Antwerp the road was fast; it seemed no time at all before they were sweeping around Utrecht and taking the road to Assen and Groningen. They had driven a hundred and ninety miles from Bruges, more or less, in under three hours and they were welcomed by the carillons ringing out eleven o'clock. There were lights streaming from the downstairs windows and as they drew up before the door, it was flung open and Al stood waiting to usher them in. Alethea, with Sarre's hand on her arm, stood uncertainly on the cobbled pavement. She seemed to have come a very long way in a very short time, but then of course she wasn't used to fast driving or the effortless manner in which Sarre conjured up meals in hotels, instant attention when he wanted it, as well as apparently having a route so imprinted on his brain that he didn't falter once the whole way.

'Welcome home,' said Sarre, and walked her up the steps.

And indeed it was a welcome home: behind Al, Mrs McCrea, Nanny, Nel and even Juffrouw Bril were grouped, and in front of them the two children in their dressing gowns but nonetheless wide awake. The hall was filled with flowers; cream roses and carnations, lilies of the valley, orange blossom and stephanotis— the flowers which had made up her little bouquet. She stood there for a few seconds, taking it all in while Sarre said something quietly to Al, who disappeared briefly and then reappeared with that selfsame bouquet. She took it with a little gasp of surprise and looked enquiringly at Sarre.

'I had an arrangement with Granny,' he told her blandly. 'You see I wanted everyone here to see just exactly how you looked at our wedding.'

Alethea had no time to reply. Everyone had surged forward to shake their hands and wish them well; the children first with hugs for their father and polite handshakes for herself, and then Al and the rest of them. And presently they all went into the drawing room, and that was filled with flowers too, with a sofa table drawn up under the windows, laden with champagne buckets and glasses. There was even a wedding cake, a masterpiece made by Mrs McCrea.

Alethea stood among them all, being toasted and

complimented on her dress and recounting the wedding to Al and Mrs McCrea while Sarre, with Sarel and Jacomina hanging on each arm, did the same for Nanny and Nel and Juffrouw Bril. It was hours later, when she was in her lovely bedroom lying awake, that Alethea recalled uneasily how the children had cold-shouldered her. She had hoped that once she was married to Sarre, they would accept her. It was still too early, she reminded herself, and turned her thoughts to her wedding. It had been a happy affair and she had enjoyed the long journey back to Groningen with Sarre. He had said that he would take her to Hamburg, that would be fun too. She slept at last, still speculating about it.

She discovered very quickly that being married to Sarre was very nearly the same as being engaged to him. True, she was now addressed as Mevrouw, and Mrs McCrea was punctilious in discussing the menus each day, as well as asking her her wishes about the running of the house.

'I'll leave that to you, Mrs McCrea,' said Alethea, going hot and cold at the idea of taking over the management of such a large establishment. 'Perhaps you would show me exactly how you go on, though. You see, you're an expert and I've never kept house in my life—all the same, I should like to learn. Could we go through cupboards and stores and so on when you have the time to spare?'

Mrs McCrea beamed at her. 'A very sensible suggestion, ma'am, if I may say so. Even if a lady doesn't run her household herself she should know exactly what goes on in it. I'll be delighted to tell you anything you want to know. And as to the menus, ma'am, if you'll just say if there's anything you don't like or would prefer…'

'I eat anything,' stated Alethea. 'Don't forget I've been in hospital for years and you get used to eating what's on your plate.'

'Ugh—you'll have what you fancy here, ma'am, you only have to say. Now, the master likes his meat— the gentlemen do, I've found, but if you fancy something lighter, that's easily seen to.'

'Thank you, Mrs McCrea. I don't know much about anything at present, but if you want something, you will ask, won't you? Pots and pans and equipment and so on, I mean. I expect you've always gone to the master for those, but it would help him if I dealt with the everyday requirements, wouldn't it?'

'Indeed it would. He has enough on his plate without bothering about the house.'

And Al took her firmly under his wing; he appeared unobtrusively with sound advice on the occasions when she found herself in doubt about something or other and he sat beside her in the Colt Sapporo which Sarre had given her. She had protested at such an expensive car and he had heard her out with his usual calm and then silenced her with the remark that as she was British she would naturally prefer a British car. 'It is for your own use,' he pointed out. 'I fully intend that you shall drive the Jaguar and the Bristol when we can get out together. But take Al with you until you have your licence.' So she drove carefully round the city while Al sat beside her regaling her with snippets of

Sarre's life, rendered all the more colourful by his cheerful Cockney voice.

He initiated her into the serious matter of the family silver, too, a collection of great age and beauty which made her eyes sparkle. 'The Guv likes it used every day,' explained Al, ''e says wot's the use of 'aving it if we ain't goin' ter use it.'

But Nanny avoided her and although the children had their lunch and tea with her each day, they remained strangers to her; always polite, always watching her. She did her best to ignore the fact and she said nothing to Sarre—indeed, when he was there too their manner towards her, on the surface at least, was friendly. All the same, she was fast coming to the conclusion that they didn't like her. And Anna—there had been no whisper of her—and no sign. For an old friend she was very reluctant to visit the house. Perhaps she and Sarre had quarrelled, perhaps Anna was upset because he had married again. Alethea longed to ask Sarre about her, but if she did he might think that she was jealous of someone he had quite reasonably called an old friend.

She had been married for just three weeks when she and Sarre were invited to dine with the *burgermeester*.

'Get yourself a pretty dress,' Sarre suggested in his kind way. 'Never mind if you're extravagant, I want you to look nice.'

So she went to town, combing the boutiques and the fashionable stores until she found something she thought Sarre would consider 'nice'. It was a pale lavender silk with a high frilled neck, long full sleeves gathered into tight cuffs, and delicate lace frills outlining its square yoke. The price made her feel quite faint, but mindful of Sarre's words, she bought matching slippers and a little dorothy bag, an extravagant trifle of lavender silk and lace to match the gown. She bore them home in triumph, deciding not to let Sarre see them until the next evening at the very last moment before they left the house. It was as well she had made up her mind to this, because he didn't come home all day and when she went down to breakfast the next morning, he had been home, Al told her, slept for an hour or so, had an early breakfast, and gone again. Alethea ate her breakfast unhurriedly, talked to the children, although they had very little to say in return, and wished that she saw more of Sarre. They hadn't been out together once, and although he was pleased to have her with him when he was home, it was never more than for an hour or two. It wouldn't have been lonely if Wienand had been there, but he was away in New Zealand, visiting his parents.

Sarre didn't come home to lunch either, and the children were gloomy and inclined to be peevish. She felt peevish herself; for some reason she had been thinking about Nick all the morning, although she had been making valiant efforts not to do so. It was silly and a little dangerous, she knew that, and if only she saw more of Sarre she might be able to forget him more easily.

Intent on cheering up the children and herself as well, she asked:

'Would you like to see the dress I've bought for this evening?'

The response was hardly enthusiastic, but she persevered. 'I'll come up to the playroom before we go, shall I?'

They agreed half-heartedly, looking at her with their inimical eyes and she thought suddenly how pathetic they were; so determined not to like her. If only she knew the reason…

But at tea time, out of doors in the garden with a tea tray on the elegant wrought iron table under the trees, they were surprisingly friendly, reminding her that she was to dress early for their benefit, asking her what jewellery she was going to wear.

That was easy to answer; she had none, only her engagement ring and the heavy gold chain she had inherited from her mother, and that wouldn't be suitable. 'But it's such a pretty dress,' she explained, 'I don't think I shall need any.'

Sarre had telephoned to say that he would be delayed, that she was to dress whether he was home or not, so she made a leisurely toilet, soaking herself in a hot bath for far too long, brushing out her newly washed hair, making sure that her nails were just right. But at length she was ready and the result, she had to admit, was more than satisfactory; her hair shone with a rich brown gloss, her make-up was just enough, excitement had given her a nice colour. She swept upstairs to the floor above, quite pleased with herself.

The children were waiting for her, and so was Nanny, who got up from her chair, giving her a look from pebble-hard eyes as she muttered a greeting, so that a little of Alethea's pleasure faded. She advanced rather awkwardly into the centre of the room, and asked: 'Well, do you like my dress?' and then added a few words in her stumbling Dutch to Nanny.

The children murmured something or other and Nanny said quite a lot, although Alethea didn't make sense of any of it. 'May I touch?' asked Jacomina.

Alethea walked over to where the little girl was standing. 'Of course—look, take some in your hand—it's silk. Perhaps Papa will buy you a dress of the same stuff—it would be pretty for parties.'

Jacomina put out a hand and caught hold of the wide skirt. 'Nanny won't let me have a pretty dress, she says it's a wicked waste for a little girl.'

Alethea glanced at Nanny and smiled, glad that she couldn't understand.

'I'm sure we can persuade Nanny to change her mind,' she observed diplomatically. 'You see, you're not a little girl any more, you know how to keep your clothes clean and I think it might be nice if you helped choose them too.'

Jacomina smiled widely. Just for a moment she forgot that she didn't like Alethea. 'Oh, may I? Would Papa mind?'

'I don't think so, I'll ask him—better still, we'll ask him together.'

Sarel and Nanny had been standing silent. What happened next took Alethea completely unawares. Sarel picked up the vase of flowers on the mantelpiece, marched across the room and threw it at Alethea's dress. Fortunately he had aimed badly; the flowers missed altogether, only the water cascaded down the front of her lovely dress.

She stood like a statue for a second or two, unable to believe what had happened, looking from Sarel to Jacomina and then at Nanny, who stood, making no effort to do anything about it. Why, she wanted him to do it, thought Alethea, she's not going to say a word. At the same instant she made up her mind what she was going to do. 'That's just the sort of thing I do myself,' she said cheerfully. 'What good luck it's only water—it'll dry, I'm sure. I'll go and see what I can do.'

She even managed a smile, a smile which she kept pinned on her face even when Sarel said roughly: 'I'm glad—I hope your dress is spoilt—I hope there's a great big stain! You won't be able to wear it... Papa will scold you...' He went a little pale. 'You'll tell Papa?'

Alethea gave him a long, considered look. 'No, I don't sneak. I know that you did it deliberately and I think that Nanny is as pleased as you are, but rest assured that I never tell tales, Sarel.'

She swept out of the room, leaving the door open and hurried back to her own room to examine the damage. It wasn't too bad, but she would have to get it dry. There was a hairdryer in the bathroom. She switched it on and with infinite care and her heart in her mouth in case it should leave a mark, dried the great wet patch. She succeeded: perhaps there was the faintest mark along the margins, but she was sure that only she could see it because she knew where the patch had been. She put the hairdryer back, just in time, because Sarre knocked on the door and came in.

He hadn't changed yet and he had only fifteen minutes in which to do so, but he showed no sign of haste. 'That's a charming dress,' he remarked, and stood to study her before crossing the thick carpet to where she stood with her back to the window. He had a flat case in his hand; he opened it now and laid it down on the dressing table. There was a necklace of Russian sapphires and diamonds inside, a delicate thing, glowing with colour. He put it round her neck and fastened it and stood back to have a look. 'Very nice. I hope you like it, my dear. It was my grandmother's. There are earrings too—are your ears pierced?'

Alethea said yes in a rather dim voice. The magnificence of the necklace had left her without words. She took the jewels he handed her and slipped them into her ears; pear-shaped drops, surrounded by diamonds, matching the necklace and ring.

'I don't know what to say,' she began. 'I've never had anything so lovely in my life before.'

He smiled. 'Grandmother would have loved you in them,' he said. 'They become you very well. Have we time for a drink before I dress?'

'No—but we'll have one.' She added with a smile: 'I think I need one—I'm a bit scared!'

They went downstairs to the drawing room and he poured their drinks. 'Is that what it is?' he wanted to know.

'What do you mean?'

'You're—er—ruffled. You are such a serene person, Alethea, but this evening something is upsetting you.'

She hadn't known that he noticed her like that. She said quickly: 'No—I'm just very excited.' She sat down in a little armchair, her silken skirts billowing around her.

'Have the children seen your dress?' he asked.

'Yes—I went upstairs a little while ago. Nanny saw it too.' It was an effort to keep her voice light, but she managed it. 'Jacomina would like a silk dress too, but Nanny thinks it's a waste for a little girl. She's quite right, of course, but do you suppose Jacomina could have one for her birthday or Christmas? Something she could choose for herself.'

Sarre looked surprised. 'Well, of course, I had no idea…' he broke off to smile warmly at her. 'You see how badly I needed a wife and the children a mother. They've got all the right clothes, I hope?'

'Oh, rather, but you know what children are; they get a taste for fashion when they're quite young these days.'

He put his glass down. 'Do exactly what you like, my dear—buy them what they want and like. If Nanny doesn't approve, I'll smooth her down.' He paused on his way to the door. 'She gets on well with you?' His eyes were very searching.

'Oh, yes!'

'And the children?'

'Everything's just fine. Will you have time to see them before we go?'

He nodded and went out of the room and straight up to the playroom.

The children were at the table, doing their homework, and Nanny was in her usual chair. There was a large damp patch on the floor near the door, and the bedraggled flowers had been thrust back any old how into the vase.

The children rushed at him and he nodded to Nanny,

who had got to her feet, looking uneasy. He enquired after their day and then asked casually:

'Who has been throwing the flowers around?'

Both children went scarlet, staring at him tongue-tied. It was Nanny who began a long rambling explanation. When she had finished, all Sarre said was: 'Well, a good thing there wasn't anything or anyone in the way.' He picked up Nero and fondled the puppy and watched his children relax. Someone had been up to something, he decided. It would be no good asking now; Nanny would only embark on another long-drawn-out fib. He bade them a cheerful goodnight and went away to dress.

The evening was a tremendous success; the *burgermeester* and his lady were elderly, kind and delighted with Alethea. They handed her round the roomful of guests as though she had been something precious and breakable, and after a few minutes of pure terror, she began to enjoy herself. Sarre stayed with her until they went in to dinner and as her partners were both middle-aged, rather learned gentlemen intent on entertaining her, she became quite easy with them, and afterwards, in the vast, grand drawing room, she found the ladies just as friendly.

They drove the short distance home in silence, but once indoors with Al hovering with coffee and the lamps alight in the drawing room, Sarre suggested that they should sit together for a little while before going to bed.

They were drinking their coffee when he remarked gently: 'You have never looked lovelier, Alethea. I'm very proud of you—you caused quite a sensation.'

'I'm glad you're pleased.' She eyed him over her coffee cup. He looked quite a sensation himself.

He got up and crossed over to where she was sitting on one of the sofas and sat down beside her. She nearly dropped her cup when he picked up a fold of her skirt. 'I'm sure no one else could see it, perhaps it's because I've been studying you so closely this evening—there's a very faint mark on your skirt—water, perhaps?' He smiled at her, his eyebrows raised slightly.

She put the cup down, unaware of the deep breath she took before she spoke. 'Oh, lord, can you really see it? I thought it had gone completely. I—I spilt some water while I was dressing—such a butterfingers— does it show very much?'

'It's almost invisible,' he assured her easily. 'So that's why you were uptight this evening.'

She was quite unaware of the relief in her face. 'Yes—I hoped no one would see it…' She looked at him. 'I hope it's not spoilt.'

He sounded positively soothing. 'Let Mrs McCrea have it; she's a wizard with catastrophes. Did she like the dress?'

Happy to be off dangerous ground, Alethea said: 'Yes, and so did Al. They're dears.'

'You've seen more of them than of me, I'm afraid. Things should be easier next week, though, Wienand will be back and I'll be able to take some time off. I have to go to Hamburg shortly, though, but remember that you're coming with me.'

She got to her feet, and he stood up, towering over her. 'I'll simply love that,' she told him, 'and it was a

CHAPTER SEVEN

LIFE WAS SUDDENLY more fun, Alethea discovered during the next week. Sarre came home each day to lunch, and once or twice he came home for tea as well, and on two evenings, after dinner, he had taken her out in the Bristol, into the country to the north of the city where it was mostly farmland and not much traffic, and handed the car over to her, sitting beside her without saying a word while she got over her initial nervousness and then, once she had discovered that the Bristol was as easy to drive as her Colt, still saying nothing when she went much too fast and narrowly missed sending them into a canal. At the last minute he had laid a hand over hers and turned the wheel and remarked on a laugh: 'You're a demon driver, aren't you? Who taught you?'

'The village blacksmith, only he doesn't shoe many horses any more.'

'You ride?'

'I used to—when I was a child before my mother and father died. And on and off since, if there was a horse which needed exercising...'

'I've got a cottage in the Veluwe. We go there some-times in the autumn—with the children, of course; they ride quite well. We might go for a week this year.'

Alethea said in a surprised voice: 'Oh, have you got another house as well as the one in Groningen?'

He said almost apologetically: 'It's really quite small, and I have to have somewhere where I can keep the horses and the children's ponies.'

Cottages and horses and ponies; he took them so very much for granted, but each one was a fresh surprise to her.

She had more surprises when they visited the solici-tor, too—a dry-as-dust old man with a bald head and pale blue eyes which were still shrewd. He received them in an office on the top floor of an old house in the heart of Groningen and offered them a glass of sherry while he and Sarre discussed money. Presently Sarre turned to her, switching to English. 'The little matter of your allowance, my dear.' He mentioned a sum which made her dizzy, and then went on to explain about wills and bequests and funds. 'And I thought that next time we go over to England we might look around for a house—we'll put it in your name, of course.'

'But why should I want a house?' she asked.

'It will all come under the marriage settlements,' he told her soothingly.

'But the children…?'

He gave her a gentle smile. 'They're already provided for.'

She said in a whisper: 'You're very rich, aren't you?' Just as though she didn't already know.

He nodded. 'I did tell you, my dear.'

'Just you—or all your family?'

'I'm afraid all the family, my dear.' He took her hand absentmindedly in his. 'You don't need to worry about it, Alethea.'

His hand felt cool and firm and she wanted to leave hers there for ever. Suddenly she knew that she would never have to worry about anything again because Sarre would do all the worrying for her; he would look after her too. A pleasant feeling crept over her and she wasn't sure what it was, but she had no chance to find out because Mijnheer Smidt began reading something out loud and presently she had to sign some papers, and when they got home the children demanded their father's attention. They needed help with their homework, they declared, and he went away with them, up to the playroom. Alethea could hear their voices and laughter echoing through the house while she sat in the little sitting room, looking through the textbooks she had been given by the nice little old lady whom Sarre had found to teach her Dutch. It would be lovely, thought Alethea wistfully, if she could have been there too, laughing and joining in the family jokes.

The children still treated her as though she were an unwelcome guest, but only when their father wasn't there, and once or twice she had caught them looking at her in a puzzled way. She had ignored that, though, trying to behave as she imagined any new stepmother would behave, never taking anything for granted, taking care not to intrude into their lives unless she was invited. Which she seldom was.

It was only a few days later when Sarre told her that he was going to Hamburg in two days' time and how did she feel about going with him.

She was brushing Rough, sitting on the lawn at the back of the house and sat back on her heels to answer him. 'Oh, Sarre, I'd love to. Shall you be there long?'

'Three or four days. I shall be at the hospital for most of the time, but we should have the evenings together. I'll drive up, it will be a good opportunity to try out the Bristol.'

'What sort of clothes shall I need?'

'Well, we may go out one evening—it's not a very big hotel, but I expect you'll want a pretty dress for dinner.'

Alethea thanked him, thinking privately that it had been a waste of time asking him, men never noticed...

'Have you got that grey thing with the patterns?'

'Grey crêpe with an amber and green pattern. Yes. Why?'

He spread himself out on the grass beside her and closed his eyes. 'I should like you to wear it.'

'Oh—all right. Does Al pack for you, or shall I do it?'

He opened one eye. 'Al rather fancies himself as a valet, you might hurt his feelings.'

She said slowly: 'I don't feel that I'm being of much use to anyone...' She wasn't looking at him, so she didn't see the sharp glance he gave her downcast face.

'You're being of the greatest use. Besides, you're not only useful, you're ornamental as well.'

She allowed Rough to wander away. Sarre looked

very placid lying there; perhaps it was the right time to ask about Anna.

'I thought Anna might have called to see us,' she said at length, keeping her voice casual.

'She sees me every day.'

'Yes, I know that,' persisted Alethea, determined to keep to the subject at all costs now she had started it. 'But you did say that she was a very old friend. I expected her to…I thought we might see more of her— she hasn't been at all.'

Sarre had his eyes closed again. 'Jealous, my dear?' he asked softly.

She flared up at once. There was no expression on his face at all, and she suddenly wanted to stir him up.

'No,' she told him waspishly. 'How could I be? One must love someone to be jealous of them.'

'You're wrong, my dear. If one loves enough, there is no jealousy.' He sat up. 'What about tea out here? The children will be home presently.'

Alethea got to her feet. 'I'll go and see Mrs McCrea—it's Al's half day, he's gone to the cinema.'

'He's a keen filmgoer. Is it too short notice if we ask Wienand and his girlfriend round to dinner tomorrow evening? He's had a lot of work to catch up on, but he tells me he can't wait to see you again.'

'I'll tell Mrs McCrea now—she loves dinner parties. Is it the same girl? Marthe?'

'Er—no. The current favourite, and I fancy the final one, is Irene, a small mouselike girl with no looks to speak of. He's known her for years—her parents are great friends of the family, but he's always

treated her like a rather tiresome small sister.' He got
to his feet and stretched widely. 'Love is no respecter
of persons.'

Alethea paused on her way. 'Do you like her?'

'Yes, she's right for Wienand.'

And Alethea had to agree with him when Wienand and
Irene arrived the following evening. Wienand greeted
her extravagantly. 'And what do you think of my Irene?'
he wanted to know when he'd finished hugging her.

Alethea smiled at the girl and put out a hand. 'What
an impossible question to answer!' she laughed, and
slipped an arm through Irene's. 'I think you must be an
angel to put up with Wienand in the first place—come
over here and tell me how you manage to do it.'

Sarre had been right, Irene was mouselike; small
and dainty with a face that just failed to be pretty and
soft brown hair, she was also desperately shy. Alethea
set herself the task of making her feel at home and succeeded so well that by the time they sat down to table
Irene was quite enjoying herself. Alethea, watching
Wienand, decided that he really was in love this time,
and with someone who would suit him very well. Irene
might be shy, but she had a lovely smile and a charming
voice and she dressed well. The evening passed off
very well and when their visitors had gone, Alethea said
in a satisfied voice: 'He's really in love with her, isn't
he—and she's a dear.'

'Matchmaking, Alethea?' Sarre sounded amused.

'No, it's just nice to see two people so happy...' She
looked away, thinking of Nick.

'You still think of him, Alethea?' Sarre's voice was as placid as usual.

'Not often.' She smiled at him. 'I think I'll go up to bed, I've a lot to do tomorrow before we go.' She wished him goodnight and went to her room, and only when she was on the point of getting into bed did she remember that she had promised Jacomina that she would ask her father if he would drop her off at school in the morning because her bike needed repairing. She slipped into her dressing gown and pattered downstairs; she hadn't heard him come up to bed, he would be in his study still.

She made no sound, although the old house creaked and sighed all around her and the tick-tock of the great Friesian clock in the hall dripped with soft deliberation into the silence. She gained the hall and slipped down its length to where she could see the study door, half open. The powerful reading lamp on Sarre's desk was on, shining on to his head and face, and she paused to look at him. He looked bone weary, every line of his face highlighted. He looked sad, too, and the sudden surge of feeling which gripped her was so strong that she stopped dead in her tracks. It was with the greatest difficulty that she prevented herself from rushing madly to him and throwing her arms round him and begging him not to look like that. It was more than she could bear, she told herself, and how could she ever have thought that she was in love with Nick when all the time it was Sarre she loved?

She stood, staring her fill at him, sitting there, unconscious of her peering at him from the darkened hall until presently, unable to trust herself to speak to him about something so mundane as a bicycle, she turned and crept back to her room where she climbed into her enormous bed, to sit up against her pillows and think what to do. Why, for a start, did Sarre look so dreadfully unhappy? Had something gone wrong at the hospital? Was he worried about a patient? Was he thinking about Anna? She shied away from the idea, but it persisted, thrusting itself into the forefront of her thoughts, so that presently that was all she was thinking about. She took a long time to go to sleep, because she had to go over all the conversations she had had with Sarre to try and find some clue, and then, tired out, she gave up worrying and allowed herself the luxury of a little daydreaming. She woke once during the night and promised herself that she would try and find out in the morning if there was something worrying him.

But when she got downstairs, a little earlier than usual because she was so anxious to be with him, she found it quite impossible. His good morning was as placid as usual, not a trace of worry was on his face, his manner towards her was just as usual, friendly. He received her request about Jacomina with perfect equanimity, wanted to know if she were ready to leave with him directly after lunch and made a few casual remarks about his appointments for the morning. With eyes made sharp by love, she studied his face covertly, loving every line of it. Whatever had been making him look like that the night before, he had thrust out of sight— her sight.

He got up to go presently, stopping to drop a swift

kiss on her cheek. She felt herself stiffen as he did so and could have wept when he drew back quickly and with a brief: 'I'll see you at lunch,' left the room, calling to Jacomina as he did so.

She was ready and waiting when he got back, with a cold lunch on the table, her overnight bag in the hall and her case in Al's care ready to load. She was wearing a new outfit, a blue patterned skirt and blouse with a little matching quilted waistcoat, and she had taken great care with her hair and face, not admitting to herself that it was a kind of insurance against the swift coolness she had felt when Sarre had left that morning. Her fault too. She need not have worried; he greeted her in his usual placid way, enquired if she would be ready to leave as soon as they'd had lunch, informed her that he had decided to take the Jaguar instead of the Bristol, and asked where the children had got to. Before she could answer him, they arrived, launched themselves at him boisterously, begged him to bring them a present from Hamburg and sat down to eat their lunch. Alethea, working away at a pleasant general conversation, found them ultra-polite, ready to answer if she spoke to them, careful to see that she had all she wanted and at the same time, just when she thought that she was getting somewhere, switching to Dutch, so that she was left out of the conversation. Never for long, of course, Sarre saw to that. She only hoped that the cold-shouldering she was getting wasn't as obvious to him as it was to her.

It was a relief to be in the car at last, with the prospect of several days with Sarre. It was exciting, and she tried not to show it too much, asking questions about their journey and his work in Hamburg, talking about the children because she sensed that he would like that, and presently, when they reached and crossed the German border, there were questions to ask about the country they were going through. They stopped for tea at a pleasant little café outside Oldenburg, half way through their two-hundred-mile journey, and soon after joined the motorway.

The Hamburg skyline was clear against the early evening sky as they neared the city; lovely slender spires and the ugly rectangles of modern buildings thrusting up into the blue above them. Alethea took her interested gaze off them long enough to look admiringly at Sarre and exclaim: 'You do know your way around, don't you?'

'I've been before—oh, several times, and I only know the main streets of the city. We're going to the hospital first, if you don't mind—it's over there, you can see it already, that large square building; it has more than a thousand beds. Then we'll go on to the hotel.'

He invited her to go in with him when they reached the hospital, but she refused nicely and was glad of it when she saw the faint relief on his face.

'I'll be about ten minutes,' he told her. 'If I'm much longer than that I'll send someone out with a message.'

He was as good as his word and Alethea jeered silently at herself for the panic she had been in until she had seen him coming unhurriedly out of the hospital again. He had two men with him, who accompanied him to the car and who were introduced as two of his colleagues, who bowed over her hand and looked her over with interest, expressing the wish that she would enjoy her brief stay. On their way once more, she waited for Sarre to tell her something of them, but his laconic: 'Well, that's settled,' seemed to be the sum of any information she could expect.

She murmured something she hoped sounded like wifely agreement and then as they reached the Binnenalster, exclaimed excitedly: 'Oh, Sarre, look, all that beautiful water and the yachts!'

'It's rather nice, isn't it? The Outer Alster is very much larger. The street we're in now is called the Virgin's Passage. In the Middle Ages it was very select; all the rich merchants lived here, and their daughters took their daily walks by the lake. It was so select that no one was allowed to carry a basket or have a dog with them. It's still considered select. There's a very good hotel here, but an even better one—much quieter and smaller—on the shores of the Aussenalster.'

He turned into a busy city street and Alethea caught a glimpse of shops before seeing the lake again, this time stretching out of sight, its banks lined with trees and grass, its smooth water ruffled by small ferry boats going from side to side, and any number of sailing boats.

'Now we're in the Alsterufer,' Sarre told her. 'It leads to the Harvestehuder Weg—the hotel's just along here, in front of the park alongside the lake.'

It looked delightful, white-painted, its windowsills ablaze with red geraniums, set amidst a formal garden. Sarre turned the car off the road into the short drive and stopped before the entrance and while a porter saw to the luggage, ushered her inside.

They had rooms overlooking the lake, and in the gathering twilight, it looked quite beautiful. Alethea, hanging over her balcony in order to watch the swans and ducks on the water, turned when Sarre spoke to her from the door.

'I'm operating in the morning,' he observed, 'and I'm afraid I shall have to go back after dinner for a consultation. Will you be all right here on your own? If you like you could go shopping in the morning—I can drop you off as I go. You'll find the shops very good, only please take a taxi back here. I hope to get away in the afternoon, but it's possible that I shan't be free until seven o'clock or thereabouts.'

She wasn't going to let him see how disappointed she was at the prospect of a whole day without him. 'I'd love to poke around,' she assured him cheerfully. 'I've been reading up a lot about Hamburg, and there's a street of little frame houses I want to go and look at.'

'The Kramer Amtsstuben,' he replied. 'I know where they are. I don't have to be at the hospital until nine o'clock. If you don't mind getting up early I'll take you there and then drop you off in the Monckeberg Strasse—that's where the shops are.'

She would at least see him for a short time; she agreed readily and, she hoped, not too eagerly, and agreed again when he suggested a stroll by the lake before they changed for the evening.

It was incredibly peaceful, right in the heart of the city and yet surrounded by trees and shrubs, the grass under their feet going to the water's edge. The sailing boats and dinghies had finished for the day, and there, by the quiet lake, they might have been miles from anywhere, only as they retraced their steps Alethea could see the lights of the city shining over the far end of the water. They stopped for a minute and she pointed across to the opposite shore. 'That looks delightful over there.' And indeed it did, the grass and the trees and beyond them the dim outlines of large villas against the sky.

'Bellevue,' Sarre told her. 'Napoleon stayed here once and remarked "*Quelle belle vue*" when he saw it for the first time, and it's been Bellevue ever since. A very wealthy neighbourhood, so I understand.'

As wealthy as the neighbourhood in which they lived in Groningen, thought Alethea wryly.

'Do you speak German?' asked Sarre casually as he took her arm and they walked on.

'*Bitte*,' said Alethea promptly, and he roared with laughter.

'One of the most useful words in the language,' he assured her, 'and you're so pretty that you don't need to know even that.'

She was glad of the gathering darkness so that he wouldn't see how red her face was. 'Oh, well,' she stammered, 'that's nice of you to say so…' and hoped he would say more, but he only suggested that it was time they returned to the hotel.

She put on a new dress, pink crêpe patterned in a deep rose, and her heart gave a little leap of pleasure at Sarre's approving look when she joined him in the bar.

It went on leaping for most of that evening, for he kept looking at her with open admiration during their dinner and said presently, when they got up to dance: 'I think I'm the envy of every man in the room, my dear.'

Alethea could have danced the night through after that, but when for form's sake she suggested that she should go to bed, he agreed so readily that she wondered if she had imagined the look on his face just because she had so much wanted him to admire her. She wished him a rather brief goodnight and only then remembered that he hadn't returned to the hospital. But he hadn't forgotten, it seemed; he had arranged to go late in the evening, so that she hadn't needed to be alone. She said 'Oh', in a startled little voice, and felt tears prick her eyelids. 'Now I feel selfish…'

He smiled down at her. 'It is I who am selfish, keeping you to myself all the evening, my dear.' He bent to kiss her cheek. 'Goodnight.'

It was a glorious morning and Alethea was up early to dress and knock on Sarre's door half an hour later. He was sitting at a small desk writing and she said at once: 'Oh, sorry—I'll go down, shall I?'

He had got to his feet at once. 'I was filling in time. I hope you slept?'

She nodded. 'And you? They didn't keep you too late at the hospital?'

He told her a little of what he intended doing that morning; a shattered arm and shoulder which he hoped to piece together again. 'Probably it will take a good deal of the afternoon as well,' he told her, 'and after that there is a foot they've asked me to repair.'

She listened carefully, deeply interested because she was a nurse, and wanting to know everything just because she loved him. But she kept an eye on the clock so that they were away in good time for him to take her to the Kramer Amtsstuben.

He parked the car by St Michael's church and crossed the road with her, to lead her down a narrow alley to the old merchants' houses, lining a small cobbled street, and looking, she supposed, exactly as they must have looked centuries ago. They had been expertly restored and although they were shops or cafés now, their charm was still very evident. Alethea went from side to side and back again, trying to see everything at once, mindful that Sarre had very little time to spare. When he looked at his watch she hurried back to him.

'I'm sorry, Alethea, but if I'm to drop you off at the shops, we must go.'

Well, ten minutes with him had been better than nothing at all, she mused beside him in the car once more, although she was out of it again in no time at all. 'Remember to take a taxi back to the hotel,' cautioned Sarre, changing gear, 'and if you're short of money, there's some in the top drawer of the chest in my room.'

He had gone, easing the big car into the morning traffic, disappearing far too quickly from her view.

Alethea shook off the feeling of being lost without him and took herself to the nearest store, where she whiled away an hour before finding her way to the pavilion by the Binnenalster and drinking a cup of very expensive coffee. She went back to the shops after that, to buy presents for the children, and her grandmother, Mrs Bustle and lastly for the staff in Groningen, an exercise which kept her busy until lunch time, when she obediently took a taxi back to the hotel, had her lunch and then went for a walk by the lake. The afternoon was as brilliantly fine as the morning had been. She walked the considerable length of the lake, keeping to the narrow path running round its edge, and then turned to hurry back, afraid that Sarre might have got back early after all.

He hadn't, of course; she was ready, dressed in the grey-patterned crêpe, when he got back, to knock on her door and ask her if she had enjoyed her day.

She told him yes, very, and how had his gone?

'Very satisfactory.' He strolled across to the bed and sat down on it. 'Everything just as it should be, provided there are no complications. I hope it will be a hundred per cent success.'

'And the foot?'

'Now that was tricky…' He went into some detail as to the operation and she listened with her usual careful attention. When he had finished, she said: 'You must be tired—do you want a drink before you change?'

'Thoughtful girl. Yes—ask them to send up a whisky, will you? What about you?' He got to his feet and stretched hugely. 'What a heavenly evening. Shall we dine later and go for a stroll first?'

She hadn't had any tea and she was starving, but that didn't matter. 'I'll wait on the balcony,' she told him, 'I'm not a bit hungry.'

There were plenty of people about, strolling along

the paths beside the lake, exercising the dog, playing ball with their children, or just walking and talking as they were. Sarre tucked her hand into his arm and explained the difficulties he had had, getting the shattered shoulder into alignment, and she listened happily. The conversation wasn't romantic, but at least they were together and he was talking to her as though he were enjoying it. It more than made up for her lonely day.

The next day followed more or less the same pattern and the one after it, and she did a little more shopping and a good deal of exploring, the highlight of each day being their evening walk together. And on the last day Sarre went with her in the morning, declaring that he need not go to the hospital until lunch time and then only briefly, and he could make a final call on their way home. And since he obviously expected her to go shopping, she hastily invented a list of presents to buy and as the morning was as beautiful as its predecessors, they walked to the Monckeberg Strasse, stopping on the way to drink their coffee in the pavilion by the Binnenalster and then strolling along by the enticing shop windows. It was in a small, expensive shop that Alethea saw a musical box, a dainty little dancing lady, exquisitely dressed in eighteenth-century costume, and when she remarked on its charm, Sarre took her inside, where they listened to its silvery, tinkling tune before he bought it for her. It was wildly expensive, even for a rich man, and she protested faintly as they left the shop, only to hear his placid: 'But I haven't bought you a present since we married, my dear.'

She thanked him again and then said, because there was a look on his face she didn't quite understand: 'I bought chocolates for the children, but I saw a game of Monopoly, do you suppose they'd like that?'

They bought that too, and more sweets for Mrs McCrea, who had a sweet tooth, and cigars for Al, who rather fancied the best brands. 'I'll collect the children's present as we go,' Sarre told her, and would say no more than that.

Alethea ate her lunch alone, for Sarre was due at the hospital at one o'clock and intended to eat there, but he was back after an hour or two and they were ready to leave by mid-afternoon. She got into the Jaguar after a last look at the quiet water; it had been a lovely few days. True, she hadn't seen very much of Sarre, but when they had been together, she had loved every second of it. They didn't speak much as he drove through the city, but as he stopped before the hospital he leaned over to open her door. 'I should like you to come in with me,' he told her.

The hospital was impressive inside as well as out. They crossed the crowded entrance hall, making their way through the visitors waiting for admission to the wards, and took a lift to the third floor. It was quiet here, a quietness explained by Sarre. 'The administrative block,' he told her. 'The various meeting rooms are here as well as the offices.' He opened a door and ushered her in to a large apartment, furnished with a long table and chairs, and half filled with people. 'Some of my colleagues wished to meet you,' said Sarre, and she began a round of hand-shaking and trivial conversation, interrupted at last by Sarre declaring that if they were to reach home that evening, they would have to leave, so Alethea went round shaking hands once more and only as they reached the door saw that he had a basket with a lid in one hand. Sarre saw her looking at it. 'The children's present,' he told her blandly as they got into the lift.

It wasn't until they were in the car that he opened the lid and lifted out a very small Siamese kitten. It curled up at once on Alethea's lap and she stroked it gently with a finger tip. 'It's adorable. Will Nero mind?'

'I don't imagine so, he'll have something to play with. They've been asking for a kitten, it's about the only animal they haven't got.'

The journey back was far too quick for Alethea. In no time at all they were on the outskirts of Groningen and she began to worry about the children and Nanny. Supposing they didn't like the presents she had brought them? Supposing Nanny refused the big box of sweets she had brought back for her?

'Why are you so nervous?' Sarre's voice sounded searching.

'Me? Nervous? I expect I'm excited,' she answered brightly. 'It was a lovely few days, Sarre, thank you for taking me.'

They had stopped before the house and he turned to her, about to speak, but the door opened and the children spilled out on to the pavement, laughing and calling to them. Alethea wondered what he had been going to say while she waited quietly until their first raptures over the kitten had died away. In the hall they stood for a few minutes while Mrs McCrea bustled up to greet them and Al went to fetch the luggage.

'What shall we call him?' the children wanted to know.

It was Sarel who shouted: 'Neptune, of course,' and when Alethea asked him why, gave her an impatient look. 'We're reading "The Little Mermaid",' he explained, as though that made everything clear.

The children were to stay up for dinner; Alethea, in her room with Nel unpacking her case, wandered round looking for the exact spot upon which to put the musical box. The little drum table near the window, she decided; it would be safe there because it was out of the way. She would let the children see it presently. She had already told them about it and they had listened politely and she had been encouraged by Sarel's: 'Did Papa buy it for you?'

'Well, yes,' she had told him carefully, 'we saw it in a shop window and I found it enchanting, so he got it for me. I shall take care of it always; it's so beautiful.'

Dinner was almost a celebration, with ice cream for the children and a good deal of talk about Neptune, now cosily asleep upstairs in the playroom with Nero, a little suspicious, but friendly enough, beside him. They went quite eagerly to bed as a consequence, thanking Alethea for her presents in polite voices, reminding her that Nanny was having her day off, so she would have to give her the sweets in the morning. Alethea watched them go upstairs and then turned away with a little sigh of relief. Everything was going to be all right; she had worked herself up for no reason at all. Even Nanny might be goodnatured in the morning. She went back to the drawing room to find Sarre on the point of leaving it. He said a little absentmindedly: 'You'll forgive me, my dear, I have quite a lot of post to read and I want to catch up on some reading.' He paused to drop a kiss on her cheek. 'A very pleasant little break,' he added, 'we must do it again some time.'

He went into his study, leaving the door open, and she heard him lift the receiver and dial a number, and seconds later: 'Anna…' She couldn't understand any more of what he was saying. She turned out the lights and went up to bed. During the last few days she had quite forgotten Anna. Half way up the staircase she paused to encourage herself with the reflection that at least the children seemed more friendly.

The bedside lamps were on when she got to her room, her nightgown was lying on the bed and her gown and slippers had been put ready. How different it was from her little room at her grandmother's house! She kicked off her shoes and wriggled her toes into the thick pile of the carpet; she would telephone in the morning and tell her grandmother about her stay in Hamburg. Sarre had suggested that later on she might like to have her stay…her thoughts were cheerful as she wandered round the room. She was brought to a sudden halt by the little drum table. The musical box wasn't on it; it was on the floor, broken and twisted as though someone had stamped on it.

Alethea picked it up slowly and saw that it was a hopeless wreck, and putting it on the table went to the window. It was open at the top but there was no breath of wind. She was closing the curtains again when Nel came in to see if she had everything she wanted and

Alethea turned a distressed face to her, and in her fragmental Dutch asked her if she had found the musical box on the floor. But Nel knew nothing about it; Alethea had known that before she asked. She wished the girl goodnight and undressed slowly. It was too late to go and ask the children and possibly a waste of time, and she couldn't tell Sarre because he would get to the bottom of the matter and that would do no one any good, least of all herself.

She got into bed and sat up against her pillows. For the first time in a long while she allowed herself to cry; first Anna, waiting at the other end of the telephone for Sarre to come home, and now the only present he had bought her broken in pieces. What was the use of a lovely home and luxury and money in her purse, although she certainly hadn't married for those? She hadn't married because she loved Sarre either, but here she was, head over heels in love with him, and what, she asked herself fiercely, was the use of that with the wretched Anna so firmly entrenched? She sobbed herself to sleep.

CHAPTER EIGHT

ALETHEA WISHED the children good morning when they got down to breakfast with her usual serenity and tried not to see the apprehension in their blue eyes, and when their father wasn't looking she had more than her fair share of glowering looks too. She wondered exactly what they would be up to next if she were mean enough to voice her suspicions as to how the musical box had got broken. She ate her breakfast with a calm she didn't feel, answering Sarre's casual remarks with a brightness which sat ill upon her pretty face, pale from her weeping, the nose still just a trifle pink despite her careful make-up, and then read her letters while he read his. They had almost finished when Sarre asked carelessly: 'And how is our little dancing lady? Did the children like her? Perhaps we should have bought one for them instead of Neptune.'

There was a chorus of dissent and Alethea was glad of it because it saved her having to answer him, but her relief was shortlived; Sarre laughed and then suggested that the musical box should be fetched there and then and the children be allowed to see it. 'Al can go up and get it,' he said easily.

Alethea's voice came out too loudly. She said baldly:
'It's broken.' She didn't look at the children, although
she was aware that their eyes were fixed on her. 'I—I
was going to tell you…I dropped it yesterday evening.'
She added rather wildly: 'I was silly enough to put it
on the little drum table by the window, I expect the wind
caught it…'

Sarre was sitting back in his chair, watching her, his
eyebrows raised just a little. He didn't comment upon
her contradiction but said in a placid voice: 'Well, shall
we have a look at it? Probably I can find someone to
mend it.' He turned to Al before Alethea could think of
anything to say. 'On the drum table in Mevrouw's
bedroom—would you fetch it, please?'

Al, who had been hovering by the sideboard with his
ears stretched, was gone with a brief: 'Will do, Guv,'
and was back again while Alethea was still trying to
decide what to say next; too late she had realised that
she had told two lies when one would have done, and
the blandness of Sarre's expression gave her the uneasy
feeling that he might have come to the same conclusion.
But his expression didn't change when Al put the poor
crushed thing on the table beside him. He picked it up,
examined it carefully and then set it down again. 'I
should hardly describe it as broken,' he observed in a
thoughtful voice. 'Pure guesswork, of course, but I
should imagine that it has been stepped on—several
times.'

He looked at the children, who sat without a word,
staring back at him. Alethea could see that they had no
intention of saying anything. What was more, she sus-

pected that Sarre wasn't going to ask them if they knew anything about it, because that wouldn't be his way; he would wait with monumental patience until they told him what they knew of their own accord. Well, three can play at that game, she told herself bracingly, and when he asked: 'What do you think, Alethea?' she said at once:

'I have no idea.' She looked at him defiantly as she spoke and he smiled a little so that she added: 'I'm very sorry…I was careless, and it was kind of you to give it to me.'

He said still thoughtfully: 'You cried about it, Alethea, didn't you?'

She had forgotten the children for the moment. She said unhappily: 'Yes, I did. You see, I…it meant something to me.'

He stared at her hard. 'Yes?' He glanced at his watch. 'I must go.' He picked up the little ruin and got up. 'I'll be home this evening, perhaps for tea, my dear.' He touched the children lightly as he left the room, but he hadn't given her the usual swift kiss she had come to expect.

When the front door had closed behind him Alethea got up too. 'Are you both ready?' she asked the children. 'It's almost time for you to go to school. Do you want me to do anything for Neptune while you're away?'

They had got up too and stood looking at her. Sarel shook his head. 'Nanny said she'd feed him.'

Alethea smiled. 'Oh, good. I'll just take Nero as usual, then. See you both after school.'

They slid from the room, looking so guilty that if she hadn't been sad about it she would have laughed, and surely Sarre, who was their father, would have seen their guilt too? She wondered what he was going to do about it and then dismissed it from her mind; she had Mrs McCrea to see, and the flowers to arrange and the dogs to take for a walk. And over and above all that she had Sarre to think about; she would have to be careful never to let him find out that she loved him, and that would mean not minding about Anna because of course if she hadn't been in love with him, Anna wouldn't have mattered at all. It was going to be horribly difficult. And what about the children? They knew that she knew that they had something to do with the destruction of the musical box. They must hate her. Her mind boggled at the future before her common sense took over; let the future take care of itself for the moment, was she not married to Sarre and wasn't he the only man in the world as far as she was concerned? She made her way to the kitchen and listened carefully to Mrs McCrea weighing the advantages of an apple torte against a dish of apple and honey moscovite. In the end they decided to have them both, with one of her renowned liver pâtés for starters, followed by Canard Sauce Bigarade, which when she described it in her soft Scots voice sounded mouthwatering as well as presenting an elegant appearance. Alethea nodded her approval and Mrs McCrea went on: 'It'll be an engagement dinner party, no doubt, ma'am, with Mr Wienand and Miss Irene coming.'

'Well, I'm not quite sure about that, Mrs McCrea, but we rather hope it will be, but nothing's been said, you understand.'

'Not a word shall be said, ma'am, though I'm sure we'll all be glad. The girls he's had, young Master Wienand, and such strange lassies. Now this one's a good girl. The master'll be glad, him being such a good man himself.' She gave Alethea a lightning glance. 'It'll be good to have a few bairns in the family again.'

Alethea went bright pink. She couldn't agree more; little brothers and sisters for Sarel and Jacomina. Heaven knew there was room enough for them in the old house and money enough to give them all they wanted. She sighed. What a frightful waste, and she would have to watch Irene and Wienand producing a family…she would have to learn to be a simply splendid aunt. She frowned so fiercely at the idea that Mrs McCrea asked anxiously: 'You approve of the duck, ma'am?'

Alethea brought her mind back to the dinner party. 'Oh, rather,' she agreed, 'and I was just wondering if we could have some bits and pieces with the sherry— those lovely nutty things you make, Mrs McCrea.'

The nutty things were a great success. The whole dinner party was a success, with Wienand at the top of his form because, sure enough, Irene had said she would marry him. She would be a darling sister-in-law, Alethea decided, watching her wrinkling her ordinary little nose over the champagne Sarre had produced, and tonight, because she was so happy, she looked pretty with colour in her cheeks and wearing a blue dress which matched her eyes. Alethea, in the grey-patterned crêpe, beamed at her with genuine delight. It was after dinner, while they were all sitting around discussing the wedding over coffee and Sarre's best brandy, that Irene said in her clear voice: 'I think that it is because of you, Alethea, that I wish to marry Wienand.' She flushed brightly. 'Oh, I would have married him, I think, but seeing you and Sarre so happy together when we were here, I thought that if you can be so content, then so can I.' She added, 'They are not alike, but they are brothers, if you see what I mean?'

Alethea thought that she saw very well and said so, which emboldened Irene to go on: 'You are not jealous?'

Neither of them had noticed that the men were listening. 'Why should I be jealous?' asked Alethea serenely.

'Well, it is perhaps…but we are going to be sisters, are we not? Wienand has taken out very many girls, but I think that he will not do so now that he has me. And Sarre, of course, he has had friends too; they did not matter, there is only Anna.' She looked apprehensively at Alethea. 'You are not angry that I speak like this?'

'Of course not.' She braced herself to utter the lie about Anna; jealousy at that very moment was rocking her so violently that she had to take a calming breath. She let it out with a rush when Sarre said quietly: 'You'll have no cause to be jealous of Wienand, Irene, just as Alethea knows that she has no reason to worry about me.' He smiled at them both. 'We've been listening quite shamelessly to you, you know. I'm glad that Alethea and I have—er—influenced you.'

They saw their guests to the door presently and stood by it in the cool evening, watching the car disappear down the street. 'She's such a nice girl,' said Alethea chattily, anxious to break the silence. 'They'll be very happy.'

Sarre flung an arm round her shoulders. 'Oh, yes, and why not? That's a pretty dress you're wearing.'

'It's getting old now,' she said shyly, 'but you said you liked it and I wanted everything to be just right for Irene…'

He seemed to understand this obscure remark. 'Yes, I know.' He sighed and took his arm away, so that she felt instantly lonely. 'I have to be at the clinic early in the morning…'

She went indoors at once. It was always the same, whenever they were together he had some good reason for leaving her. She said now in a colourless voice: 'It was a lovely evening. Will you be in to lunch tomorrow?' She was already walking ahead of him, making for the stairs.

'No—tea, perhaps. Alethea…'

She cut in ruthlessly, longing to stay with him but determined to get away as quickly as she could. 'I'll say goodnight, then.'

She flew up the staircase without even looking at him.

She was in her dressing gown, brushing her hair, when she saw the musical box. It was on the drum table and she stared at it unbelievingly.

When she picked it up she wasn't certain if it was the same one, miraculously repaired, or another one just like it. It didn't matter; Sarre had done it for her, he must have known that she had been upset.

She flew from the room and across the gallery and knocked on his door, the dainty thing held carefully in one hand. Sarre was standing in the middle of his room in his shirtsleeves, taking off his tie. His: 'Yes, my dear?' was quite unsurprised.

'Sarre, my little dancing lady—I found her. You did it, didn't you? You never got her mended?'

'Yes, I did. There's an old instrument maker who sees to my instruments and is an expert in repairing the irreparable. He spent the day on her.'

She blinked back tears. 'Oh, Sarre, how can I ever thank you? You don't know…after my carelessness… that you should have bothered.'

He was leaning against a tallboy, his hands in his pockets, staring at her. He said deliberately: 'You can show it to the children now.'

She said a little breathlessly: 'Yes, of course—they'll love it.' She edged towards the door. 'Well, thank you again, Sarre. I really did mind about her being broken.'

He left the tallboy and came towards her. 'Yes, I know that.' He took the musical box from her and set it down. 'I find it quite encouraging.' He swept her close and kissed her hard, put the toy back into her hand, and opened the door. 'Sleep well,' he said.

Alethea got ready for bed, wondering what he had meant. Why should he find it encouraging that she had minded? And he had kissed her…he'd kissed her before, of course, but this time it hadn't been a cool peck on one cheek. Perhaps he had felt sorry for her. She wound the musical box and sat listening to its tinkling tune; she would have to play it for the children in the morning and

not betray her feelings for one second, but there was no
one to watch her now, no blue van Diederijk eyes staring
at her. She played the tune again, snivelling like a small
girl.

But there was no sign of that at breakfast the next
morning. She set her treasure on the table and without
looking too closely at the children's surprised faces,
wound it up, talking about it all the time, and when it
had finished its tune, she enquired after Neptune and
Nero, reminded the children that it was their swimming
lesson that morning, observed that it looked like rain
and somehow contrived not to offer a cheek for Sarre's
duty kiss. After the way he had kissed her last night, she
wouldn't be able to bear it.

She went about her chores presently, having her
daily chat with Mrs McCrea, peering into the linen cupboards, paying a visit to Nanny, who received her with
tight-lipped courtesy and stood by while she played
with the kitten and collected Nero for his walk with
Rough, and that done, she went along to the small room
at the back of the house where she had her daily Dutch
lessons now. It was a dear little room; rather cluttered,
because everyone used it and it had a lovely view of the
garden. Alethea spent an hour struggling with the
simple sentences which would help her most, at least
to begin with, and then thankfully bade her teacher
goodbye and wandered into the drawing room. It was
then that she realised that she hadn't seen Al all the
morning.

Mrs McCrea, busy with the making of a Dundee
cake, looked at her reproachfully. 'You only had to pull

the bell rope, ma'am,' she pointed out, 'there's no call
for you to come all this way. Is it something you want?'

'Only to ask about Al—he doesn't seem to be here…
he's not ill?'

There was a little pause. 'He's got his day off,
ma'am. Is there anything Nel can do in his stead?'

Alethea picked up a handful of almonds and
munched them. 'Oh, no, thank you.'

'It must have slipped his mind to tell you,' observed
Mrs McCrea comfortably.

It was at lunchtime that the children told her that they
couldn't find Neptune. They looked at her so accusingly
that she guessed at once that they supposed that she had
hidden him in revenge for smashing the musical box.
She said with deliberate calm: 'No, I haven't taken
him; he was safe in the playroom when I was there this
morning and I haven't been there since. Of course I
know that you smashed the musical box; I expect you
had some reason for doing it, but I don't intend to tell
anyone, nor do I intend to take revenge—certainly not
at the expense of a kitten.' She went on bracingly: 'Now,
who saw him last? Was he alone for any length of time?
Did anyone leave the door open?'

'Nanny said he was there asleep—she had to go
down to the kitchen for something and when she got
back she can't remember if he was there or not.'

'Then probably he's in a cupboard.' Alethea glanced
at the clock. 'Look, if we hurry over lunch, we'll have
half an hour before you have to go back to school; we'll
search the house, room by room—perhaps Nanny will
help us.'

They stared at her silently and she added gently: 'Look, I'm on your side, you know,' and was rewarded by the speed with which they polished off their meal.

The search disclosed nothing, at least nothing of Neptune. True, a ball which had been missing for months came to light in a great chest on the landing outside the playroom, and a pair of woollen mitts which Jacomina had been missing since the winter were found in the pillow cupboard in the hall. By the time the children had to go back to school, they had peered and poked into almost all the house; there were still the kitchens, the drawing room and their father's study, but Alethea said that she would take a look there and then search the garden. She hoped devoutly that she would find Neptune in the house, because it was pouring with rain and the gardens were quite large with potting sheds, wheelbarrows and the like, all of which would have to be searched.

But there was no sign of him indoors; it had taken a long time to look around the drawing room and even longer in the kitchens, even with the help of Mrs McCrea and Nel. There was nothing for it but to search the garden. But first Alethea decided to go back to the playroom and make sure he hadn't turned up.

For once Nanny didn't scowl at her, but shook her head, and Alethea crossed to the window to look unhappily at the teeming rain outside. It was the faintest possible movement in the big ash tree which towered close to the house wall outside the playroom which made her throw up the window and lean out. She couldn't see anything, what with the rain whipping the hair round her face and the wind blowing, but she was almost sure that she heard a faint mew. It was quite possible that Neptune had gone on to the windowsill and jumped the short distance from it into the tree. She wondered if she dared to do the same thing, and decided against it. She hadn't climbed a tree in years and it wasn't something she enjoyed doing, but Al wasn't there, Nel had gone home for the afternoon and Mrs McCrea was hardly the build...

She managed to convey to Nanny where the kitten was and went downstairs. Slacks first and something to tie up her hair, and gloves in case Neptune took exception to being rescued. She went to the kitchen next to tell Mrs McCrea, but since that good soul was having a doze by the Aga, Alethea hadn't the heart to wake her, so she scribbled a note on the kitchen pad and went out of the back door.

For a summer day, the weather was shocking. She bent her head to the wind and the rain, gained one of the sheds, found a short ladder and carried it to the ash tree, where she found that it reached only half way up its great trunk. She would have to stretch upwards and pull herself up to a higher branch. She wasn't very good at it; it took several attempts before she was actually astride one of the lower branches, and now she could see Neptune, clinging to a much smaller branch above her head, his fur in spikes, his eyes like saucers. She would have to climb higher.

That took a long time too, or so it seemed and now she was up there, she wasn't so keen on heights. She forbore from looking down and wondering how she was ever going to reach the ground again, and concentrated on getting hold of Neptune. She managed that too, more by good luck than skill, for the little creature slipped and as he hung she was able to catch hold of him.

But now how to get down? She took one horrified peep below her and then averted her eyes. She would need both hands for a start, so where was she to put Neptune? She had on a thick sweater over her slacks, but it had no pockets. She would have to stay where she was; Mrs McCrea would wake up and someone would come and look for her; Nanny knew where she was. She looked up hopefully, but the leaves were too thick and she could see nothing, and unless Nanny had the window open, which she strongly doubted, no one would hear her shout. But she did shout all the same, just in case. Nanny might hear.

Of course Nanny didn't, but all the same her powerful cries were heard; she nearly fell off her branch when Sarre let out a bellow below her.

'What the hell are you doing up there?' he wanted to know, and she was so surprised to hear the rage in his voice that she didn't answer for a few seconds.

'Neptune's up here—I've got him safe, but I'm not sure how to get down.'

She heard what sounded like a rumbling laugh. 'Just stay where you are,' commanded Sarre. 'I'm coming up.'

He was obviously better at climbing than she was. He was there, close beside her, within seconds, and while she was still wondering what they would do next he had scooped Neptune up and tucked him inside his jacket. 'Now come down,' he told her. 'You can't fall, I'm right behind you and you'd have to knock me over first. Let go of that branch, you can't take it with you. Now catch hold of that stump and let yourself slide.'

If Alethea hadn't been so breathless with fright she would have rounded on him; ordering her about in such a callous fashion when she was petrified! She set her teeth and did as she was told. After what seemed aeons of time Sarre said: 'Here's the ladder, stretch out your left foot.'

She slid it cautiously downwards and felt the rung beneath her shoe. Which was all very well, but that foot was stretched to its utmost and the rest of her was sprawled on the tree trunk.

'You can't fall,' said Sarre's patient voice, 'I've both feet on the ladder and my arms are stretched on either side of you.' He sounded amused. 'Have you got your eyes closed?'

'No, but I wish I had.' She lowered herself a few inches and felt Sarre right behind her, he felt a bit like a tree trunk himself and she suddenly didn't mind any more, and when he said abruptly: 'Jump now,' she did so, landing neatly in his arms.

He didn't let her go at once, and she stayed squashed up against him, listening to the steady thud of his heart and Neptune's urgent mewing. She could have stayed there for ever, rain and all, but after a few moments Sarre let her go and hurried her in through the kitchen door to be met by Mrs McCrea and Nanny. He handed the kitten to Nanny with directions to dry and feed him and then turned to look at Alethea.

'All right,' she said crossly, 'I know I look quite awful.'

Sarre laughed, 'I think you look rather nice,' and kissed her wet face. 'Run along and get into a hot bath and then come and have tea in the study. I've some work to do, but I can drink my tea at the same time.'

Normally she would have stayed in the bath for hours, now she was in and out again in minutes, deciding what to wear. Sarre had never asked her to have tea with him before while he worked. It smacked of intimacy, a cosy state of married bliss…she put on a linen dress of pale green, did her face and her hair and skipped downstairs.

Mrs McCrea was coming out of the study as she went down the hall and she thought the housekeeper looked put out. She called: 'I'll be down presently, Mrs McCrea,' as she tapped on the door and went in.

Sarre was at his desk. He had changed his wet clothes for slacks and a cotton sweater and he had a pen in his hand and a pile of papers before him. Sitting opposite him was Anna, talking in a low urgent voice.

Alethea stopped short, disappointment swamping her, so that she found it difficult to speak. 'So sorry, I didn't know you were busy.'

She smiled brightly, looking just above their heads and backed out again, although Sarre had got to his feet and was saying something. Let them have their tea, she told herself savagely, and raced upstairs to the playroom where Neptune, quite himself again, was lying in his basket while Nanny mounted guard over him. She was still there when the children came home and she stayed where she was, on the floor beside the kitten while Nanny talked at length.

Sarel came over to her at last. 'Nanny says you rescued Neptune from the tree. Thank you.' He sounded polite but unfriendly.

She got to her feet; she wasn't wanted here either. 'That's all right, I'm glad he's OK. Will you have your teas up here? Your father's working in his study.'

It was Jacomina who answered her. 'Yes, we know, we went to see him. Doctor Anna's there too.'

Back in her room Alethea sat down and wondered what she should do. Go downstairs and have tea by herself? Share it with the children? They wouldn't like that. She got up slowly and fetched her bag and went to find Mrs McCrea.

'I'm going out for a little while,' she told her. 'I want to match up some embroidery silks.'

Mrs McCrea nodded; the shops had been shut half an hour or more, but she wasn't going to say so. Alethea wandered off and after a little while stopped and had coffee at a café in the city and then wandered on again. She went so far that she had to take a taxi back to be in time for dinner.

She went to say goodnight to the children first and then went down to the drawing room. Sarre was standing by the window, but he came towards her as she went in. 'You didn't come and share my tea,' he observed mildly.

'No. You had Anna to share it instead.'

His face took on the bland expression which she recognised covered any feelings he didn't want to show. 'So I did. There was tea enough for three, though.'

'Two's company, three's none,' she reminded him flippantly.

'In that case Anna is the third.'

Alethea had missed her own tea and strong feelings were bubbling over inside her. She said snappily: 'No, she's not. I am.' She added: 'After all, that's what I expected.'

She watched his face change. The blandness was still there, but his eyes glittered with what she felt sure was rage. 'Are we quarrelling?' he asked her in a voice so cold she could hear the ice tinkling.

'Why not?' she asked a little shrilly. 'At least you might notice me…' She raced to the door. 'I'm not hungry, I think I'll go to bed.'

By the time she had torn off her clothes and had another bath, she was famished as well as frightened at what she had said. She had been stupid shouting like that; now Sarre wouldn't be just casually friendly, he'd begin not to like her. She cried herself to sleep worrying about it.

He had gone when she got down to breakfast in the morning. Only the children were still at the table. They wished her good morning and looked at her wan face with some curiosity. They looked doubtful too, and she couldn't think why—and really, she thought wearily, it didn't matter; they had made up their minds not to like her and they showed no signs of changing them. She drank her coffee, saw them off to school and went into the garden. It was beautiful and peaceful there; she felt better after a while and went in search of Mrs McCrea.

'Isn't Al back?' she asked when they had settled the meals for the day.

'He'll be here before lunch,' declared Mrs McCrea. She volunteered no further information, so presently Alethea took the dogs for their walk while she pondered over the situation between herself and Sarre. Well, it was hardly that. Sarre wasn't an easy man to quarrel with, he just stood there looking horribly calm; it was like hitting her head against a feather bolster.

It was still damp from the rain in the park although it was a glorious morning; mindful of muddy paws, she took the dogs round the little *steeg* which led to the garages and the back garden gate and went into the house through the kitchen, drying the dogs on the way. 'I'll bring up the coffee presently,' Mrs McCrea told her. 'Nel's busy upstairs.'

'I'll come down for it,' offered Alethea. 'It's only me to have it—my teacher doesn't come this morning.'

'I'll bring it all the same, ma'am,' said the house-keeper in much the same sort of voice that Mrs Bustle used when she disapproved of something Alethea wanted to do, so that she took herself out of the kitchen, the dogs running ahead of her. As soon as she opened the service door they began to bark. Sarre was in the hall, sitting on one of the marble-topped wall tables; they rushed at him and he fended them off gently as he got up.

'Hullo,' said Alethea, and then searched around for something else to say. To plunge into an apology for the previous evening seemed a little premature, besides, she had no idea what she would say. 'Have you forgotten something?' she asked brightly.

'No, I find myself with a couple of hours to spare. Shall we have coffee in the garden?'

She had the absurd notion that he was laughing at her. 'Yes, why not? It's a lovely day. I've just taken the dogs…' What a silly remark, she thought vexedly, and turned with relief as the front door opened and Al stood back to admit someone.

'Granny!' screamed Alethea, and hurled herself at her elderly relative.

'Yes, dear,' said Mrs Thomas, straightening her hat. 'It is I. Sarre sent Al to fetch me—just for a couple of days, you know.'

'Sarre,' Alethea had turned to look at him, 'how kind of you! I can't begin to thank you… Mrs McCrea said Al had a day off…'

'Well, so it were, as one might say,' said Al cheerfully. 'Keep it dark, says the guv; so off I creeps at first daylight an' 'ere we are, all safe and sound.'

'Oh, Al!' Alethea smiled at him because she was too excited to say more. 'Sarre, you never said a word…'

He only smiled and spoke to Mrs Thomas. 'Shall we have coffee in the garden first, then Alethea can take you to your room.'

Sarre went back to his rooms shortly afterwards. He had patients to see, he told them, and a hospital round in the afternoon, so he wouldn't be home until the evening. 'You can have a good gossip,' he told them, looking hard at Alethea.

But when later her grandmother asked her if she were happy, she found she couldn't talk about it very easily. She described her life, dwelling on the luxury in which she lived, she skimmed over the children, who had appeared at lunch and behaved like angels, but she had a little more to say about Nanny but nothing about Sarre. When she had finished her grandmother sat back in her chair.

'Yes, dear, and now supposing you tell me all about it.'

Alethea dissolved into tears, something she hadn't meant to do. 'Oh, Granny, I'm so hopelessly in love with him and there's this awful Anna…'

She talked about Anna at some length and her grandmother listened carefully, tutt-tutted at the end and remarked dryly: 'You're his wife, my dear.'

Alethea agreed unhappily. 'Yes, I know, but there are the children…' She explained about them too. 'They hate me,' she declared, 'and I've tried so hard, Granny; they're darlings and they're Sarre's, so I love them…'

'Love is a great deal stronger than anything else,' pronounced Mrs Thomas. 'Just bear that in mind, child.'

The visit lasted two days, no longer because Mrs Thomas said that she couldn't leave Mrs Bustle for longer than that, but Alethea crammed a good deal into it. She took Mrs Thomas on a sightseeing tour in her Colt, conducted her round the house, accompanied her shopping, and made sure that she saw as much of Sarre and the children as possible. The children liked the old lady and she liked them, and when Mrs Thomas suggested that they might like to spend a few weeks with her later on, they were wildly enthusiastic. Just as enthusiastic as Sarre was about having both his grandmother-in-law and Mrs Bustle over for Christmas. And on the last evening of Mrs Thomas's visit, they had guests for dinner, Wienand and Irene and Anna. Sarre had suggested her casually, with his eyes on Alethea, who instantly said: 'Oh, yes, of course we must have Anna,' and volunteered a good deal of information about her, just as though she hadn't already done so. Sarre had smiled a little and contributed nothing to Alethea's eulogy. He had treated her with unfailing courtesy since their unhappy conversation about Anna and even if Alethea had wanted to bring the matter up it would have been difficult.

Arrogant man, thought Alethea crossly. Just like him to decide that no more would be said on either side, without giving her a chance to utter a word.

She wore a new dress that evening; the colour of honey, quite beautiful and wildly expensive. But at the end of the evening, when the house was quiet and she had time to think, she came to the conclusion that she might just as well have worn an old sack and she was still seething inwardly from Anna's playful: 'Why, Alethea, you're getting plump.'

She had replied suitably and, she hoped, with suitable lightness, furious to see Sarre's lips twitch. It had helped a little when her grandmother remarked that it was a good thing, because she had always been too thin. 'Such a big girl,' she told the assembled company. 'I don't hold with beanpoles.'

Sarre had agreed with her and everyone had laughed, and Alethea had felt like the fat woman at a fair. She had, she considered, behaved beautifully, even when Anna had kissed Sarre in greeting and again when she left; better than little Irene who had looked worried and embarrassed.

Alethea got up from the window seat where she had been sitting and kicked a fallen cushion quite viciously round the room; it relieved her feelings enormously. And she wasn't getting fat; she took a good look at herself in the bathroom looking-glass to make sure.

She felt lost and lonely after her grandmother went home, especially as Sarre went to Amsterdam on the same day. Probably, he told her, he would have to spend the night. She had looked at him blankly and asked stupidly: 'Must you—stay away?' and when he had said quietly that he thought it might be better to drive back to Groningen in the very early morning, she had cried much too loudly: 'Of course you'll have Anna with you.'

His face, usually so placid, had shown anger, but all he said suavely was: 'No, but when you make remarks like that, Alethea, I'm tempted to do so.'

He had left the house then and she had mooned around until Mrs McCrea had asked her if she would mind going to the grocers' for her. There was still an hour left till lunch and the children's return from school; she gathered together her smattering of Dutch and went upstairs to talk to Nanny. It was high time she asserted herself over various matters. Her Dutch might not have been very grammatical, but she certainly got the gist of her wishes over to Nanny; in future she would take the children shopping for their clothes and when they were naughty they were to be punished—not severely, but enough to make them realise that they had done something wrong. And Nanny wasn't to shield them from punishment, either.

'You don't love them,' declared Nanny.

'Oh, yes, I do—I want them to grow up like their father, Nanny. You love them, but you spoil them.' She hoped she had the right words; she had looked them up earlier. 'You haven't helped me, have you? I should like to be friends…'

'You wish to take my place,' Nanny snorted. 'Never, *mevrouw*!'

'Of course I don't want to take your place, why should I and how could I? The children love you, you fill a gap.' She said hole because she didn't know the Dutch for gap and anyway her Dutch was beginning to peter out. But Nanny seemed to understand. She looked surprised and then pleased before her face resumed its usual disapproving look.

The children were unusually talkative at lunch, telling a rather involved story about a cottage, uninhabited now, which had at one time belonged to Nanny. 'It's not far from here,' said Sarel, 'in the Langestraat, there's a *steeg* on the left. We've always wanted to go there, but Papa won't let us because he says it's dangerous.' He eyed Alethea thoughtfully. 'Why is it dangerous?'

'I don't know,' observed Alethea, only half listening, 'but if your papa says it is and you mustn't go there, then you must obey him.'

'We could go and look at it from the outside.' Sarel gave her a quick look.

'Well, no, I don't think that's a good idea, I'd much rather you didn't.'

'We obey Papa, but we don't have to obey you,' muttered Sarel.

Alethea paled a little. 'No,' she said steadily, 'I don't suppose you do unless you want to. All the same, please wait until your papa gets home—he'll be here tomorrow.'

She managed to smile at them both; Sarel looked defiant, but Jacomina looked scared and shamefaced.

She saw them off to school presently, reflecting ruefully that she hadn't done much good, either with them or with Nanny.

She took the delighted dogs for a long walk that afternoon, getting back much later than usual. The children would have had their tea, which was perhaps just as well. She had hers in the little sitting room, planning something to do that evening. The children missed their father when he was away, she knew that; perhaps if they were quick with their homework, they could all go to the cinema, there was a Disneytime film on... She went upstairs and found Nanny alone and when she asked where the children were, she got a blank stare and a spate of Dutch she couldn't follow. She gave up presently and went down to find Mrs McCrea who would probably know, but she didn't know either.

'Their pa's away,' she commented severely. 'That Nanny's a dear good woman and dotes on them, but they twist her round their thumbs.'

Alethea went uneasily to her room. It was almost seven o'clock and they never stayed out as late as that unless they were with friends and someone knew where they were. She went to the window and looked out and then glanced round the room. There was an envelope propped up against the musical box and she was across the room like a flash to open it and read.

Sarel's written English was peculiar but understandable. They had gone, he and Jacomina, to explore Nanny's cottage. That was all. Alethea was out of the room and shutting the front door behind her within seconds—she hadn't been listening very well to what Sarel had told her about the little house, but she could remember the name of the street and he had said that it was close by. She didn't know why she was so scared. True, the children had been gone for two hours and that was a long time, but it wasn't only that. Sarre had forbidden them to go there, so probably it wasn't safe.

She had to stop and ask several people how to get to Langestraat and when she did reach it she wasn't very impressed. It was narrow and old and most of the cottages in it were condemned, and in the *steeg* they were even worse; some of them already tumbled to the ground. Sarel had said something about it being on a corner and sure enough there it was, its windows boarded up although most of the boards had been carried off long since. Alethea tried the door and found the key in the lock as she pushed it slowly open.

The little place was a ruin indeed, with plaster all over the floor from the walls and ceiling, broken floorboards and a gaping hole where once the stove had stood. It was filthy dirty too and smelled dreadful. She picked her way from the tiny hall and down a few broken stairs to the kitchen at the back where it was almost dark because the only little window was completely covered over. She held the door open behind her and called in what she hoped was a normal voice, then jumped out of her skin when she heard Sarel answer.

His voice quavered a good deal and sounded hollow, quickly explained when he told her that they had both fallen into the cellar below the kitchen. 'I dropped the matches and we couldn't see, and there isn't a stairs any more, so we fell…'

Alethea stood just where she was. 'Are you hurt, my dears?'

Their shouts were reassuring. 'Then hang on, I'll pull you up.'

She had moved cautiously as she spoke and saw in the furthest corner the dark hole which should have been the cellar stairs. She got down on her knees and peered over the edge and caught a glimpse of the two faces below. Rather a long way down, but if she could find a chair and pass it down to them and they stood on it… The door behind her banged shut and left her in almost complete darkness. It just needs a rat or two, she thought wildly, and asked with all the calm she could muster if Sarel knew where the matches had been dropped. Somewhere in the middle, he told her vaguely, so she crawled around on her hands and knees on the filthy floor until she found them. The box wasn't full, she had used almost all of them before she found a broken old chair in a corner. She picked it up with a triumphant cry and it fell to pieces in her hands. She had to tell Sarel, of course, who suggested that she should go for help. 'We'll be all right,' he assured her in a voice that sounded as though he needed reassuring rather badly, and certainly she could think of nothing else to do; it would be a waste of time to wring her hands and moan if only they had a light…

The door had jammed, but after a good deal of furious kicking on her part it gave way and she ran up the rickety little stairs to the hall. The door was shut, locked, and she had left the key on the outside. And this time it didn't yield to her blows and thumps. It took a little while for her to admit that it was useless and when she tried the only window she couldn't make any impression on the boards. She went back slowly to the children and explained. 'I'm a fool to leave the key outside,' she told them, 'but at least when someone comes they'll be able to get in.'

'Who'll come?' asked Jacomina tearfully.

Alethea remembered that she had put the note they had written in her pocket and she hadn't seen anyone before she left the house; probably no one would come. 'Your papa,' she said with loud conviction.

'But he's in Amsterdam.'

'I know, but he might come back this evening.' It was a forlorn hope; he was much more likely to stay away after what she had said to him.

'I'm coming down,' she called cheerfully. 'We might as well be together.'

There were no matches left. Alethea crept cautiously towards the top of the non-existent stairs and lowered herself very slowly, terrified out of her wits. She dangled for a few seconds, feeling nothing below her. 'Sarel,' she called in a carefully calm voice, 'can you stretch out a hand and touch me? Come carefully, and then both of you get as far away as you can while I jump.'

She felt his fingers brush her shoe a moment later and heard the children creeping away. 'I'm coming now,' she called, and jumped. She landed on a pile of rubbish which slipped and slithered away from her feet as she scrambled upright. 'Can you come over here?' She was ashamed of her shaky voice. 'I think it would be better if we kept together, but first I'm going to explore a bit.'

The children reached her and she touched them reassuringly before making her way inch by inch away from them. Once or twice she tripped over piles of stone and bricks and twice she found herself up to her ankles in water. She remembered that a great many houses were built on piles driven into the water; perhaps the piles were giving way...as though to answer her thought the ground shifted under her feet and there was a wet, sucking sound and the rattle of stones falling into water. She tried not to hurry back to where the children were, panic catching at her throat that even in that small space she might put a foot wrong and go the way of the stones.

The children's hands were cold but somehow welcoming. Alethea put an arm round each of their shoulders and said cheerfully: 'Well, here we are, I don't think we had better move, it's a bit wet here and there. What shall we talk about while we're waiting?'

'Will Papa be long?' asked Jacomina, and gave a great sob.

'I don't know, my dear, but he'll come—I'm sure of that.' And she was.

Sarel's voice had changed; it was friendly. 'I think

he'll come too. It's our fault, Alethea—we came here on purpose, we wanted you to come and we were going to lock you in just for a little while. I—I'm sorry, and so's Jacomina, you mustn't be angry with her. She's always liked you and I think I did too, only I didn't want to, so we pretended we hated you…'

Alethea squeezed his shoulders. 'I'm not angry with either of you,' she assured him warmly. 'I used to play pranks when I was a little girl, and this is only a prank.'

'No, not really, but it's nice of you to say so.' His voice was very earnest and put her in mind of Sarre. 'You're sure Papa will come?'

'Positive.' She had read somewhere that if one thought hard enough about someone they would think about you. Well, she was thinking very hard about Sarre and miracles happened. Jacomina began to cry and Alethea bent down and kissed her. 'Let's talk,' she said hearteningly. 'Let's talk about Christmas and what we'll do then and the presents we'll buy, and I'll tell you about the hospital…' She had a momentary picture of Nick; what would he have done in such a situation? she wondered, and found that she didn't care in the very least. She took a deep steadying breath. It was beastly down there in the dark, but at least the children were safe and she was absolutely certain that Sarre would come. She began to tell the children just how an English Christmas pudding was made.

CHAPTER NINE

SHE HAD LOST all count of time when Sarre's voice, calm, almost placid, said from somewhere above them: 'I'll have Jacomina first—lift her up as high as you can, Alethea, and you, *liefje*, put your arms above your head so that I can catch your hands.'

He waited while Alethea, dumb with relief and happiness at the sound of his voice, got cautiously to her feet and lifted the little girl. It was difficult for the rubble underfoot shifted to and fro with every movement and Jacomina was quite heavy, but she managed it at last and felt her weight lifted from her aching arms as Sarre lifted his daughter to safety.

'And now Sarel...'

A cold hand came out of the dark and clutched at Alethea's. 'Papa, I will go last—it is not kind to leave Alethea here alone in the dark; she's a girl.'

Alethea gave the hand a squeeze. The conditions were hardly ideal in which to make friends, but they seemed to have managed it. Sarre's voice was unhurried. 'Spoken like a man, Sarel, but I need you up here to look after Jacomina—she's scared.'

Alethea spoke carefully from a mouth dry with fear.
'Yes, your papa's right, Sarel, and Jacomina always
does as you say.'

The sweaty little hand returned her squeeze and
withdrew. 'I'm heavy…'

'Isn't it lucky I'm tall?' she reassured him, and
steadied herself on the rubble once more and braced
herself to lift him. It was far worse than Jacomina; she
thought that her arms would break in the few seconds
before Sarre caught Sarel's upstretched arms and
hauled him up beside him. But she forgot the pain in a
rush of panic. It was hideously dark and the loose stones
were shifting under her feet again. If Sarre wasn't quick
she might disgrace herself for ever and scream. She
swallowed terror as best she might as he spoke again.

'Scared, Alethea?' His voice was warm and reassuring. 'We'll have you out in a few seconds now, just do
exactly as I say.' She lifted her aching arms above her
head and tried not to think of the emptiness below her.

'And when I say so, jump, my dear.'

'Jump?' her voice rose. 'I can't—oh, I can't!
Suppose you don't catch my hands? I'm lower than the
children were.' Somewhere below her the rubble slid
and settled again. 'Sarre, I'm frightened.' Her voice,
which she had managed to keep steady until now,
wobbled badly.

'Of course you're frightened,' his voice soothed her,
'but I'm not going to let you go, that's a promise. Now
take a nice deep breath and when I say so, jump. Do as
I say, Alethea.'

His calm had rubbed off on to her—besides, he had

promised. When he said 'Now!' she jumped, her arms stretched to their utmost, and felt the stones beneath her scatter as she did so.

His hands were like iron bands round her wrists, her arms were being pulled from their sockets.

'Relax, my dear,' said Sarre in a perfectly ordinary voice, and then began to haul her up inch by inch, working his hands slowly up her arms until they were below her elbows. She hung like that for a second or two while he pulled himself to his knees and then to his feet and then swung her up and out to hold her close in his arms. He was breathing hard and his heart was pounding. She could feel it under her ear; it was comforting and made her feel safe again. When he asked harshly: 'Are you hurt?' she mumbled into his shoulder that she was fine, fighting a desire to have a good howl.

'The children?' she asked then.

'Over in the corner.' The torch he was holding suddenly went out. 'Damn!' He let go of her and fished out his lighter. Its tiny flame made the horrible bare little room even more horrible, but by its light Alethea had seen something—candles in two broken-down enamel candlesticks. She flew across the room and carried them back to Sarre and when he had lighted them held them triumphantly aloft, debating where to set them. She heard Sarre saying something, but she wasn't attending; she was elated at their escape and all she wanted now was to find a safe place for their lighting so that they could get out of the house as quickly as possible. There was a shelf against one wall, sound enough still. She put them down and asked him: 'What did you say?'

He was kneeling by the children, making sure that they weren't hurt, but he turned to speak over his shoulder. 'I said "By Sun and Candlelight," Alethea.'

Something in his voice made her look at him, but although she knew vaguely that it was from some poem or other, she couldn't be bothered just then to think about it. 'Are the children all right?' she asked.

'I believe so—bruised and a cut or two. And you?'

'Never better,' she lied cheerfully; her arms ached so much she could hardly move them, but if he stopped to examine them now they would never get away. There was an ominous rumble from somewhere beneath them and Sarre said: 'I think it's time to go.' He blew out one of the candles and picked up the other and gave a hand to Jacomina who was snivelling unhappily. 'Sarel, stay close to Alethea and right behind me.'

They negotiated the rickety stairs safely and gained the narrow passage, and Sarre opened the door and blew out the candle. The evening was still bright. Jacomina, catching sight of the scratches and bruises on her small person, broke out into fresh sobs. Sarel didn't look much better, but it was Alethea who had come off worst; she had cut her hand quite badly when she had jumped down to the children, her tights were in tatters as well as her dress and her hair was full of dust and cobwebs and over and above that her arms, where Sarre had hauled her up, were already an angry red. And as for Sarre, he hadn't escaped scot free either. He had taken off his jacket the better to rescue them and his shirt was torn and stained. Once in the dreary little alley, he tossed the jacket into the back of the car, lifted

Jacomina, still howling, into the back seat, told Sarel to get in after her, and opened the door for Alethea. One glance at her and he picked her up and tossed her gently into the seat beside his: 'You look all in,' he murmured, 'your arms must be painful.'

She mumbled that they were all right without looking at him and sat silent while he drove home. Only when they were within sight of the house did she ask: 'How did you know?' She stirred to ease her aching legs. 'Where we were…'

'I didn't, at least not for a time. I tried all the usual places—the children's friends, your friends, anywhere that Nanny and Al suggested, and then I remembered hearing Sarel talking about the old cottage which had belonged to Nanny. It was a shot in the dark…'

He stopped the car and got out, and at once the house door flew open and Al, closely followed by Nanny and Mrs McCrea, came down the steps.

Sarre had picked up Jacomina after he had helped Alethea out of the car and handed her over to Al, then led the procession back into the house.

'Hot baths,' he ordered, already halfway up the staircase with his daughter. 'I'll look you over afterwards, and give Mevrouw some brandy, Al, she's in need of it.'

He had disappeared as he spoke and Alethea was sat down tenderly in one of the chairs in the hall and made to drink the brandy while Sarel stood close by, looking anxious and describing with a wealth of detail to Nanny and Mrs McCrea just how awful it had been. Al took the glass away presently and said: 'Now, ma'am—upstairs to your room, like the guv says.'

She felt peculiar and a little sick, but she managed to say: 'Sarel, you'll do what Papa says, won't you? A bath and then jump into bed so that you can be properly looked at.' She managed a smile. 'You were a brave boy,' she told him, 'and thank you for wanting to stay behind in that awful place.'

He said something then to send her spirits soaring. 'I wished to do what your son would have done.' He grinned at her, looking exactly like his father so that her insides melted. 'I shall call you Mama.'

She thanked him and then turned away quickly before he should see the tears pouring down her dirty face.

She had a good cry in the bath so that by the time she was sitting obediently in a dressing gown while Sarre examined her hurts, she was admirably composed once more. True, her eyes were dreadfully red, but he wasn't likely to notice that; she had washed her hair and even done something to her face, happily unaware that it had in no way disguised the fact that she had had a good howl. Her arms were swollen now and the redness was turning purple, but the ache was better, she assured him as he closed the cut on her hand with butterfly plasters, gave her an ATS injection and then gently removed some grit from one eye. 'Are the children all right?' she asked once again.

'In splendid shape. Nanny's giving them their supper and then they're going to their beds. They want to see you before then if you could manage it. I've asked Mrs McCrea to throw away our dinner and get us some supper instead.' He touched her cheek gently. 'You are a very brave girl, my dear, we are all deeply in your debt.'

Alethea wanted to catch hold of his hand and hold it against her cheek for ever, but all she said was: 'The children were splendid, you must be proud of them.'

He said slowly: 'What did you think about while you were waiting down there?'

It was on the tip of her tongue to say, 'You,' but that would never do. 'Oh, the children, and I made plans for Christmas although it's a bit early for that, and whether Mrs McCrea would make an extra chocolate cake because the children have friends coming to tea on Saturday. We talked a lot, too—I told them about Theobald's…'

His voice was so soft she hardly heard it. 'And did you think about Penrose?'

It seemed a funny question for him to ask, but she answered it at once. 'Well, yes as a matter of fact, I did—I tried to imagine what he would have done if he'd been there.' She laughed a little. 'He didn't…' She wasn't given the chance to finish what she had intended to say—that he hadn't even seemed real to her, certainly she wouldn't have been so sure that he would come to their rescue—Sarre interrupted her: 'I've been very selfish.' He was bending over her arm, feeling the bones gently. 'Why don't you go to England for a week or two, visit your grandmother and look up your friends at Theobald's?' His voice was very level.

She gave him a surprised look and felt her heart sliding down into her slippers. He wanted her out of the way—probably she bored him stiff when they were alone together; indeed, she reflected, that must be the case, for they were so seldom alone nowadays. Pride

stiffened her, it stiffened her voice too. 'I'd love that—
just for a few days. Would you mind if I did?'

She wasn't looking at him, and only heard his voice,
bland and impersonal. 'Not in the least.'

They had their supper presently, fussed over by Al,
each course served with an urgent message from Mrs
McCrea that they were to eat all of it. They talked about
the evening's happenings and Sarre told Alethea that he
had already telephoned and arranged for the ruined old
place to be boarded up and locked. 'Before someone
else does the same thing,' he explained. 'I can't think
what got into the children…' He sighed. 'I suppose
they will have to be punished.'

'No, please don't—I expect it was curiosity, you
know what children are, and they were so frightened,
that was punishment enough.'

'Very well, if you say so, my dear. Presumably in their
own good time, I shall discover the right of the matter.'

Sarre discovered it sooner than he had expected.
Alethea had gone upstairs and wished the children
goodnight and although they had begged her to stay and
talk she had kissed them fondly, pointed out that their
father had said that they were to stay in bed and go to
sleep, and promised that they would all have a nice talk
in the morning. She had barely regained her own room
when they were out of bed and, dressing gowned and
slippered, on their stealthy way down to their father's
study.

Sarre was sitting at his desk when the children
knocked on the door, and although he had said that
they were to go to bed some hours earlier, he didn't look

surprised. His 'Hullo there,' was cheerfully welcoming as he waved them to a big armchair opposite the desk. But the children refused.

'We must stand, Papa,' declared Jacomina. 'We have things to tell you.'

'I thought perhaps you might.' Sarre switched to Dutch. 'Go ahead, then. Sarel…?'

'It's about Alethea. It was our fault that she was with us in the old cottage. You see, we wanted to frighten her.' He paused and his father begged him to go on with an impassive face.

'And suppose you begin at the beginning,' he suggested.

'We didn't want a mama. We thought that we were quite happy without one, Papa, and when you told us about Alethea we said that we wouldn't like her, so we did not try to be friends with her.' He added in a small voice, 'We were not rude exactly, but she wanted to be friends and we did not allow ourselves to like her. Only then she didn't mind about Caesar in her bed and she didn't tell anyone either, and she found Neptune for us and she was kind, but we still did not want her for our mother. Anyway, she wasn't like a real mother, more like a visitor, for she sleeps always alone, not like our friends' mothers and fathers, and they kiss good morning and laugh together and…' He stopped because Sarre was looking so grim.

'Go on, Sarel.'

'And then we made this plan—to frighten her just a little so that she would go away, although I think we didn't really want her to go, only we'd said that we weren't going to like her. So we went to Nanny's old cottage and left a note for her and of course she came after us. We thought we'd just lock her in for a little— just for fun…' He faltered under his father's eye. 'But when we got inside it was dark and the floor gave way and we fell into that cellar.' He shivered. 'It was so very dark, Papa. And then Alethea came and she didn't make a fuss or tell us we'd been naughty, but tried to get us out, and when she couldn't she said she would go for help, only she'd left the key on the outside of the door and it banged shut so that she couldn't get out. So she said she'd climb down to us and see if she could get us out. She found an old chair, but it broke when she tried to stand on it and she said that would be no use, so she jumped down. She was very brave, Papa.'

'Just like a mama,' wailed Jacomina in a tearful voice. 'She told us stories and talked and said if we had patience you'd come. We all had to keep very still because when she jumped she fell in some water and the floor started moving. Papa, we want her to stay with us for always and be our mama. We are very fond of her and we are sorry that we have been unkind to her.'

'We would like her to stay, do you wish that too, Papa?'

Sarre's eyes gleamed beneath their lids, but all he said in his calm way was: 'I think that tomorrow morning you must go to Alethea and tell her just what you have told me and ask her if she will forgive you and stay with us all.'

Sarel asked uncertainly: 'You are angry, Papa?'

'Not with you, *jongen*.'

Alethea was sitting up in bed, drinking her morning tea and fighting a headache while she examined the livid marks on her arms, when there was a tap on the door and the children entered.

She had thought just for one lovely moment that it was Sarre, but she hid her disappointment quickly and bade them sit on the bed. 'Would you like some tea?' she asked, conscious that the atmosphere was heavy. 'There are a couple of tooth glasses in the bathroom.'

They shook their heads, looking so glum that she said: 'What is it, my dears?' At the same time she pushed the little plate of tiny biscuits Mrs McCrea had made specially for her between them. It was Jacomina who began, only to dissolve almost immediately into a series of snivels, so that it was Sarel who embarked on the long, rather incoherent tale; how they had made up their minds before they had even seen her that they would not like her. But somehow it hadn't worked, Sarel admitted, a little red in the face. 'You didn't mind about Caesar and you never told anyone either, and you found Neptune and you never told when I spoilt your new dress—not even when Papa asked.' His voice became urgent. 'Please will you stay with us? We should very much like to be your children if you'll have us.' He gulped. 'We don't want you to go away, ever.'

Alethea forgot about her stiff arms; she put them round both children and hugged them close. 'Oh, my dears,' she cried, 'you don't know how happy you've made me. I shall so enjoy having a son and daughter— we're going to be very happy!'

Jacomina smiled at her from a blotchy face and Sarel

grinned. 'Oh, super!' He ate a biscuit and Jacomina ate one too. Alethea was so happy that she recoiled only slightly when Caesar's ratty face appeared from under Sarel's pyjama sleeve. She recovered at once and gave him such an enthusiastic greeting that Sarel insisted that the beast should sit on her hand. She bore this high honour with fortitude until the children went away to dress, bearing Caesar with them, much to her relief.

She was drinking another cup of tea to restore her nerves when there was a second tap on the door. Surely this time it would be Sarre?

It was Nanny. She came and stood by the bed and burst into speech, repeating herself so often that Alethea managed to understand her quite well. Nanny was deeply sorry for her manner towards Mevrouw. She hoped that she wouldn't be sent away, if Mevrouw could understand that she loved the children. She had been a wicked old woman and only now did she realise how wrong she had been to reject Mevrouw's kindness and friendship.

Alethea caught her hand and held it, frowning over her Dutch, anxious to get it right. 'And they love you, Nanny. You must never leave us, it's unthinkable— you're important to them and we trust you, you must know that.' She paused to dig up a few more words. 'If I had been you,' said Alethea, 'I should have done exactly the same thing.'

She leant up and kissed the old woman's cheek. 'Friends,' she said.

Two difficult tears rolled down Nanny's cheeks. 'Friends, Mevrouw,' she repeated, 'for always.'

It was still quite early. Alethea got up and dressed
and went downstairs to find Sarre and the children
already at their breakfast. Sarre got to his feet at once.
'My dear, I expected you to stay in bed…'

'I'm not ill, thank you,' she gave him a sunny smile,
'only sore.'

The children rushed to get her coffee and toast and
she watched his mouth curve in a faint smile although
he didn't say anything, only presently he excused
himself with the information that he would be home for
lunch and perhaps they could have a little talk then.

Alethea agreed happily; her day was perfect, or
almost so. Nothing would be perfect of course unless
Sarre loved her, and as he wasn't likely to do that she
would have to make the best of a bad job, but to have
the children's affection was something…and Nanny.
She felt as though she had conquered Mount Everest.

Her state of euphoria lasted until lunchtime when
Sarre came home, inspected her cuts and bruises, pronounced them satisfactory and then, over lunch,
informed her that he had her tickets.

'My tickets?' Alethea gaped at him. She had quite
forgotten all about his suggestion that she should go to
England; indeed, she hadn't really taken it seriously, only
agreed with it out of pique. She said now, a piece of toast
poised halfway to her mouth: 'You weren't serious?'

He nodded. 'By boat—you prefer that, don't you?'

'But Sarre, I can't go—I simply can't—you must see
that. The children you, know. They—want me.' She
smiled suddenly at the mere thought. Somehow it made

her relationship with him much closer now that his children had accepted her.

'But I want you to go, Alethea.' He smiled at her, but she could see the arrogance in his face, she saw the tiredness there too. He looked much older, she discovered with a shock; it must have scared him badly when the children had disappeared, although he hadn't shown it.

'Why?' she asked him baldly.

'Need we go into that? I think we both know the reason. I know that the children are important, but this is even more so—how could you ever be completely happy?' He stared at her. 'I'm right, am I not? You aren't happy, even though the children have admitted at last that they're fond of you.'

She had put the toast down and was staring at her plate. 'No, I'm not,' she mumbled, 'but I don't want to go. And even if I went…' she drew a deep breath. 'You do want me back, Sarre?'

His smooth: 'That's entirely up to you, Alethea,' didn't reassure her in the least. All the fight went out of her in the face of his bland impassiveness. 'I'll telephone Granny,' she said.

He glanced at her. 'Yes, do, my dear. I got tickets for the day after tomorrow, but if that doesn't suit you, I'll get them changed.'

What did it matter when she went? He didn't want her in his home; she had thought just lately that he liked her a little, not just as the other half of a friendly arrangement between them, but as a girl. She must have been wrong. Perhaps it was Anna after all; if it was she wouldn't be able to bear it.

They finished their lunch, talking about nothing that mattered, and she saw him out of the house as she always did when she was home and went back to the sitting room to think. She would have to discover some way of staying; she had no idea what, but she had two days in which to do it.

The two days came and went. Alethea had tried several times to talk to Sarre, but somehow he had no time; the telephone rang or he was on the point of going out or he had urgent work to do. She saw him off to the hospital on the day of her departure, still without having a chance to talk. But he would be home for lunch; she knew that, it wasn't operating day and he had an out-patients clinic in the afternoon. She would see him at lunch. She had planned it carefully; the children were going to a friend's at midday, so she would have him to herself. She answered their anxious questions as to just when she would be coming back with a cheerful-ness which wholly deceived them, begged them to be good children and do as Nanny told them and not to annoy their papa, and kissed them with a secret sorrow that it might be a long time, perhaps never, before she saw them again.

She stood on the steps waving them goodbye on their way to school. Perhaps she was being gloomy. Sarre might let her talk; if it was Anna, then she could tell him that she wouldn't interfere. She rehearsed what she was going to say as she did her last-minute packing, had a talk with Mrs McCrea and Nanny and then went into the garden.

She was arranging the flowers she had picked when

Al came to her with a message from Sarre to say that he wouldn't be able to get home to lunch after all, that Al would take her to the station in his stead, and that he hoped she would have a good holiday. Alethea stood with the scissors in her hand, staring at him. 'But he can't!' she cried. 'Al, are you sure that's what he said?'

Al nodded. 'Ho, yus, ma'am.' He eyed her knowingly. 'It ain't ter yer liking, neither, eh?'

She put the scissors down carefully, rammed the flowers in an untidy bunch into a priceless Sèvres vase and took off her gardening gloves.

'No, Al, it isn't quite…I'm a bit disappointed.' She turned her back to pick up a dropped flower and when he asked if she would have her lunch on a tray in the sitting room she said yes, that would do, thank you, and waited until he had gone before she turned round.

She was so unhappy that she was past tears. Sarre could have telephoned, not sent that cold, polite message. He hadn't wanted the embarrassment of saying goodbye, she supposed, or to give her the chance of talking to him. She looked at her bruised arms and wondered how he could have been so gentle with her when he treated them, if he was so utterly indifferent to her. He was a kind man; perhaps he thought it kinder to let her go without seeing her again.

She wandered out into the garden again. What had she said or done in the last few days to make him so determined to send her away? She had thought he would have been pleased to see how happy the children were with her; she had never said a word to him about them, or about Nanny, but he must have noticed how the children had changed towards her…

She wasn't going to be able to bear it any longer. Half way up the staircase she stopped to look up at one of Sarre's ancestors, a handsome man who must have had the girls eating out of his hand. 'I shan't come back,' she told him. And she meant it.

She made a pretence of eating the lunch Al served so carefully and then because it was time to go, she went upstairs to put on the jacket of her new outfit, a charming skirt and blouse in honey-coloured crêpe-de-chine not in the least suitable for travelling. She had changed it at the last moment, because she had made up her mind to see Sarre before she caught the train and she wanted to look her best. She went to the dining room next and poured herself a glass of brandy; she loathed the stuff, but she needed something to make her brave enough to tell him that she wasn't coming back, and more than that, that she loved him and that was why.

She felt a little peculiar as she got into the car. Everyone had crowded into the hall to say goodbye and hope that she would be back soon, and she had time to beg Nanny to look after the children and to tell Mrs McCrea to make an extra large cake for the weekend. And once in the car, beside Al, she told him to go to the clinic first. 'I'll be very quick, only a few minutes,' she explained. 'There's something I want to tell…that is…'

'Cor, lummy, ma'am, yer don't 'ave to explain, I ain't that feeble in the 'ead. The guv ain't 'alf lucky, 'aving yer ter love 'im.' Which left her speechless.

The forecourt of the clinic was crowded. Alethea asked Al to let her out at the entrance before finding a parking space and hurried in through the swing doors. The outpatients' department was full but not as full as all that. Surely Sarre would be able to spare her a few minutes; besides, Doctor Jaldert was there too. She crossed the tiled floor to the desk. The nurse on duty there was a stranger to her and when she asked to see Sarre she was told politely that no, that wasn't possible, not for at least an hour or more.

'But I'm his wife,' explained Alethea. 'I know he'll see me—besides, there aren't very many patients.'

'I'm sorry, Mevrouw van Diederijk, it isn't possible—it has nothing to do with the patients.'

Surely Sarre hadn't given instructions that he didn't want to see her? But he didn't know that she would be coming… Alethea fought an urge to burst into tears. 'Would you let him know I'm here?' And if she had to go on much longer, she thought wearily, she would run out of her meagre, quite dreadful Dutch.

The nurse answered her with stony politeness. 'That is also not possible, *mevrouw*.'

Something went pop inside Alethea's unhappy head. She got up from the seat the nurse had begged her to take and before that astonished young woman could do anything about it, had marched to the nearest door and opened it. What was more, she told herself as she did so, she would open every door in the place until she found him. That her recklessness was due to the brandy she had drunk before she left the house to give her courage she chose to ignore.

She had the first door open before the nurse reached her. She was aware of her urgent voice in her ear but she didn't listen. The room was a large one with a long table down its centre; round it sat a number of soberly clad gentlemen, and at its head was Sarre.

Alethea shook off the nurse's restraining hand and began a march up the room, to be met almost at once by Sarre, who had leapt from his chair to meet her. She said in a rather loud voice because of the brandy: 'Sarre, I have to speak to you—now.' She smiled at the gentlemen because she was feeling better now that she had found him. 'I'm sorry if I'm interrupting something. The nurse tried to stop me…'

Sarre's hand was on her arm. He looked as though he wanted to laugh, although not a muscle of his face moved. 'Supposing we go to my office, my dear?' He spoke quietly and then raised his voice a little in order to address their audience, who murmured in answer as he swept her out of the room.

It was very quiet in his office. He offered her a chair and went to lean against the back of his great desk, his hands in his pockets. 'And what do you wish to tell me, Alethea?' he asked her very gently. 'Something which necessitated you having a go at the brandy bottle…'

She said defiantly: 'I'm not very brave, but it's all right now I'm here. Sarre, I thought I could go without telling you, but I can't, so Al said he'd bring me here so I could see you on the way to the station.'

'So Al knows?'

She got out of her chair; she felt better standing. 'Well, he guessed.'

Sarre took a hand out of a pocket and inspected his nails. 'And I'm to be told too, or must I guess as well?'

'You wouldn't guess in a thousand years,' declared Alethea in a voice squeaky with emotion. 'I'm not coming back, Sarre.'

He put his hand back into his pocket and looked at her. 'I wondered if you had intended that. It hasn't been all roses for you, has it? The children—oh, don't look so surprised, I have eyes in my head and my hearing is excellent—besides, they came and told me all about it. But it's too late, perhaps—they've discovered that they're very fond of you, they wanted to go to England with you, did you know that? just so that they could be sure that you would come back here. And Anna—I have been at fault there. I wanted to tease you a little to arouse your interest, make you jealous, but now I don't suppose you will ever believe me if I tell you that we're friends and nothing more and that she plans to get married to a childhood sweetheart.' He sighed. 'And Nanny—oh, she's your slave now, like every other member of the household, but at the beginning she was eaten up with jealousy; and there is Penrose. You have every right to leave me—us, Alethea.'

'None of those things matter,' said Alethea, hurrying a little so that she could say what she had to say and go. 'I'd never have left you for any one of them; they'd have all come right in the end...'

'But this—whatever it is—won't?'

She had taken her gloves off and was twisting them ruthlessly into a shapeless suede ruin. 'No.' It was astonishing how difficult it was to get the words out. They came in a rush finally. 'It's so silly of me; I've fallen in love with you, Sarre. You'll find that hard to believe after Nick…but of course I've never been in love before, only thought I had—it's quite different.'

Sarre spoke very quietly. 'Yes, it is, isn't it? I have thought myself in love a dozen times, and that includes my first wife, but when I fell in love with you, I knew that none of them counted—only you, my darling.'

Alethea dropped her gloves and stared at him with her mouth open.

'You're in love with me? You never said so.'

'I was afraid to. You see, I wasn't sure about young Penrose. Once or twice I very nearly told you that I loved you and each time something prevented me. I knew I'd have no peace until you had been back and seen him…'

He left the desk and caught her close so that her very ribs ached. 'Do you remember when I hauled you out of that cellar? There was a candle…'

She interrupted him in a little rush of words. 'You said "by sun and candlelight", but I didn't understand…it's Elizabeth Barrett Browning, isn't it? "I love thee to the level of every day's most quiet need, by sun and candlelight…" Do you really, Sarre?'

He bent his head and kissed her without answering and it really was far more satisfactory than words. Presently she lifted her head. 'All those men…'

'A meeting—a medical committee meeting, my dearest, not in the least important. What have you done with Al?'

'He's outside, waiting. Sarre, do the children really want me for their mama?'

'Oh, yes, indeed they do. What is more important, I want you for my wife.'

She leaned up to kiss him. 'What about Granny?'

'There's the telephone, my love; we'll let her know as soon as we get home.' He kissed her again. 'We'll go now.'

Al was waiting, sitting patiently reading the *Daily Mirror* behind the wheel. He got out of the car as soon as he saw them, gave them a quick look and said in a tone of deep satisfaction: 'Goin' 'ome, are we? Now that's what I calls a 'appy ending. It'll be the champagne tonight, eh, Guv?'

Sarre had his arm around Alethea's shoulders. 'Right as usual, Al, champagne for everyone.' He smiled at his faithful old servant. 'I'll take Mevrouw van Diederijk home with me. Bring yourself home, will you? And take the luggage indoors and see that someone unpacks it. Thanks.'

It was a beautiful late afternoon. He tucked an arm under Alethea's and crossed the forecourt to where the Jaguar was parked. Halfway across he stopped and looked her over. 'That's new,' he declared, 'and I like it, my darling. Were you dressed to kill?'

She looked up into his quiet, loving face. 'No—I felt like someone going to the guillotine and making the best of themselves…'

He smiled slowly. 'You're very beautiful.' He had his hands on her shoulders and she said hurriedly:

'Oh, darling Sarre, you can't—not here.'

'Can't I?' he asked her, and did.

CHAPTER ONE

CHASE TRANSFERRED his gaze to the road and identified a foreign spot on the horizon. A car. Almost half a mile away, where the straight, tree-lined drive met the public road. He could tell it was coming too fast, but judging the speed of a vehicle moving straight toward you was tricky.

It wasn't until it was about two hundred yards away that he realized the driver must be drunk...or crazy. Or both.

The guy was going maybe sixty. On a private drive, out here in ranch country, where kids or horses or tractors or stupid chickens might come darting out any minute, that was criminal. Chase straightened from his comfortable slouch and waved his hands.

"Slow down, you fool," he called out. He took the porch steps quickly and began walking fast down the driveway.

The car veered oddly, from one lane to another, then up onto the slight rise of the thick green spring grass. It just barely missed the fence.

"Slow down, damn it!"

He couldn't see the driver, and he didn't recognize this automobile. It was small and old, and couldn't have cost much even when it was new. It was probably white, but now it needed either a wash or a new paint job or both.

"Damn it, what's wrong with you?"

At the last minute, he had to jump away, because the idiot behind the wheel clearly wasn't going to turn to avoid a collision. He couldn't believe it. The car kept coming, finally slowing a little, but it was too late.

Still going about thirty miles an hour, it slammed into the large, white-brick pillar that marked the front boundaries of the house. The pillar wasn't going to give an inch, so the car had to. The front end folded up like a paper fan.

It seemed to take forever for the car to settle, as if the trauma happened in slow motion, reverberating from the front to the back of the car in ripples of destruction. The front windshield suddenly seemed to ice over with lethal bits of glassy frost. Then the side windows exploded.

The front driver's door wrenched open, as if the car wanted to expel its contents. Metal buckled hideously. Small pieces, like hubcaps and mirrors, skipped and ricocheted insanely across the oyster-shell driveway.

Finally, everything was still. Into the silence, a plume of steam shot up like a geyser, smelling of rust and heat. Its snake-like hiss almost smothered the low, agonized moan of the driver.

Chase's anger had disappeared. He didn't feel anything but a dull sense of disbelief. Things like this didn't happen in real life. Not in his life. Maybe the sun had actually put him to sleep....

But he was already kneeling beside the car. The driver was a woman. The frosty glass-ice of the windshield was dotted with small flecks of blood. She must have hit it with her head, because just below her hairline a red liquid was seeping out. He touched it. He tried to wipe it away before it reached her eyebrow, though, of course that made no sense at all. Her eyes were shut.

Was she conscious? Did he dare move her? Her dress was covered in glass, and the metal of the car was sticking out lethally in all the wrong places.

Then he remembered, with an intense relief, that every good medical man in the county was here, just behind the house, drinking his champagne. He found his phone and paged Trent.

The woman moaned again.

Alive, then. Thank God for that.

He saw Trent coming toward him, starting out at a lope, but quickly switching to a full run.

"Get Dr. Marchant," Chase called. "Don't bother with 911."

Trent didn't take long to assess the situation. A fraction of a second, and he began pulling out his cell phone and running toward the house.

The yelling seemed to have roused the woman. She opened her eyes. They were blue and clouded with pain and confusion.

"Chase," she said.

His breath stalled. His head pulled back. "What?"

Her only answer was another moan, and he wondered if he had imagined the word. He reached around her and put his arm behind her shoulders. She was tiny. Probably petite by nature, but surely way too thin. He could feel her shoulder blades pushing against her skin, as fragile as the wishbone in a turkey.

She seemed to have passed out, so he put his other arm under her knees and lifted her out. He tried to avoid the jagged metal, but her skirt caught on a piece and the tearing sound seemed to wake her again.

"No," she said. "Please."

"I'm just trying to help," he said. "It's going to be all right."

She seemed profoundly distressed. She wriggled in his arms, and she was so weak, like a broken bird. It made him feel too big and brutish. And intrusive. As if touching her this way, his bare hands against the warm skin behind her knees, were somehow a transgression.

He wished he could be more delicate. But he smelled gasoline, and he knew it wasn't safe to leave her here.

Finally he heard the sound of voices, as guests began to run around the side of the house, alerted by Trent. Dr. Marchant was at the front, racing toward them as if he were forty instead of seventy. Susannah was right behind him, her green dress floating around her trim legs.

"Please," the woman in his arms murmured again. She looked at him, the expression in her blue eyes lost and bewildered. He wondered if she might be on drugs. Hitting her head on the windshield might account for this unfocused, glazed look, but it couldn't explain the crazy driving.

"Please, put me down. Susannah… The wedding…"

Chase's arms tightened instinctively, and he froze in

his tracks. She whimpered, and he realized he might be hurting her. "Say that again?"

"The wedding. I have to stop it."

* * * * *

Be sure to look for TEXAS BABY,
available September 11, 2007,
as well as other fantastic Superromance titles
available in September.

HARLEQUIN®
Super Romance®

Welcome to Cowboy Country...

TEXAS BABY

by *Kathleen O'Brien*

#1441

Chase Clayton doesn't know what to think.
A beautiful stranger has just crashed his
engagement party, demanding that he not
marry because she's pregnant with his baby.
But the kicker is—he's never seen her before.

Look for TEXAS BABY and other fantastic
Superromance titles on sale September 2007.

Available wherever books are sold.

HARLEQUIN®
Super Romance®

**Where life and love weave together
in emotional and unforgettable ways.**

REQUEST YOUR FREE BOOKS!

2 FREE NOVELS PLUS 2
FREE GIFTS!

From the Heart, For the Heart

YES! Please send me 2 FREE Harlequin Romance® novels and my 2 FREE gifts. After receiving them, if I don't wish to receive any more books, I can return the shipping statement marked "cancel." If I don't cancel, I will receive 4 brand-new novels every month and be billed just $3.57 per book in the U.S., or $4.05 per book in Canada, plus 25¢ shipping and handling per book and applicable taxes, if any*. That's a savings of over 15% off the cover price! I understand that accepting the 2 free books and gifts places me under no obligation to buy anything. I can always return a shipment and cancel at any time. Even if I never buy another book from Harlequin, the two free books and gifts are mine to keep forever.

114 HDN EEV7   314 HDN EEWK

Name _____ (PLEASE PRINT)

Address _____ Apt. _____

City _____ State/Prov. _____ Zip/Postal Code _____

Signature (if under 18, a parent or guardian must sign) _____

Mail to the Harlequin Reader Service®:

IN U.S.A.: P.O. Box 1867, Buffalo, NY 14240-1867
IN CANADA: P.O. Box 609, Fort Erie, Ontario L2A 5X3

Not valid to current Harlequin Romance subscribers.

Want to try two free books from another line?
Call 1-800-873-8635 or visit www.morefreebooks.com.

* Terms and prices subject to change without notice. NY residents add applicable sales tax. Canadian residents will be charged applicable provincial taxes and GST. This offer is limited to one order per household. All orders subject to approval. Credit or debit balances in a customer's account(s) may be offset by any other outstanding balance owed by or to the customer. Please allow 4 to 6 weeks for delivery.

Your Privacy: Harlequin is committed to protecting your privacy. Our Privacy Policy is available online at www.eHarlequin.com or upon request from the Reader Service. From time to time we make our lists of customers available to reputable firms who may have a product or service of interest to you. If you would prefer we not share your name and address, please check here. ☐

HR07

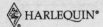